Liz was go

His baby.

Liz, who was t
ever met, who was the woman he loved, was
going to have his baby.

Elation battled horror.

From the moment he'd been diagnosed with
his Multiple Sclerosis he'd known he'd never
have any children. How the hell could he have
known he'd already fathered a baby?

How could he have a child when he'd only be
condemning the child to a father with a disease
that had the power to demand everything?

To have loved her, never wanting to hurt her,
to keep from being a burden to her, he sure
was doing a wrap job on Liz.

He'd told her he didn't love her on the night
she'd intended to tell him about their baby.
In his mind he'd had a clear idea of what the
right thing was—for him to set Liz free.

Her pregnancy changed everything.

She'd need him more than ever.

Oh, hell.

What had he done?

Janice Lynn has a Masters in Nursing from Vanderbilt University, and works as a nurse practitioner in a family practice. She lives in the southern United States with her husband, their four children, their Jack Russell—appropriately named Trouble—and a lot of unnamed dust bunnies that have moved in since she started her writing career. To find out more about Janice and her writing, visit www.janicelynn.com

Recent titles by the same author:

THE DOCTOR'S MEANT-TO-BE MARRIAGE
THE HEART SURGEON'S SECRET SON
THE DOCTOR'S PREGNANCY BOMBSHELL

SURGEON BOSS, SURPRISE DAD

BY
JANICE LYNN

⊚ MILLS & BOON®
Pure reading pleasure™

First published in Great Britain 2008
Paperback edition 2009
Harlequin Mills & Boon Limited,
Eton House, 18-24 Paradise Road, Richmond, Surrey TW9 1SR

© Janice Lynn 2008

ISBN: 978 0 263 86828 9

Set in Times Roman 10½ on 12¼ pt
03-0209-44840

Printed and bound in Spain
by Litografia Rosés, S.A., Barcelona

SURGEON BOSS, SURPRISE DAD

To my fabulous editor Lucy Brown.
Thanks for all you do to make me a better writer.

CHAPTER ONE

ASHES to ashes. Dust to dust.

The preacher's words blurred in Liz's mind like a hazy cloud.

She couldn't believe Gramps was really gone, that she'd never again look into those twinkling sky-blue eyes, never hear him call for his "Liza girl" or hear his laughter. Not ever. A tear slid down her cheek.

Not that there had been much laughter over the past two years. There hadn't. Gramps's congestive heart failure had seen to that. His condition had been worsened by dementia near the end and she'd never known if she'd see recognition in his eyes or not. But those occasional glimmers, those few lucid moments had kept her going.

As much as her heart ached that he was gone, as much as she'd miss him, relief also washed over her. Never had she begrudged caring for her grandfather. Goodness knew, he'd cared for her when no one else had. But working full time as a registered nurse and coming home to relieve the hired nurse each night wore on a person's resolve, their sleep, their mental and emotional state. Still, she'd have done it endlessly if it had meant Gramps getting better.

Only he hadn't, and she'd known that no matter how much she did, she'd only been delaying the inevitable. Each day she'd seen him slip further away from the vital man he'd once been. She'd watched him long for death and eventually let go to the disease that had claimed his life.

Thank goodness for Adam. Without him she'd never have stayed sane these past few months.

Dr Adam Cline had been by her side, understanding when she'd cut their dates short if Sara, Gramps's hired nurse, had called, understanding why she hadn't been able to stay the night at his place, understanding why their relationship could never progress. She'd promised Gramps she wouldn't put him in a nursing home as long as she could care for him, and she hadn't. Somehow between she and Adam they'd managed to keep him at home.

She'd never expected Adam to take on the care of her seriously ill grandfather, but in many ways Adam had. He'd been wonderful.

Was wonderful.

She glanced at the tall, dark-haired man sitting next to her on the hard wooden pew. His strong fingers held her trembling ones while the preacher continued his moving eulogy. Her heart pinched at the tenderness with which Adam's thumb caressed her palm in gentle, comforting circles.

She squeezed his hand, hoping to convey how much it meant that he was at her grandfather's funeral. He'd confessed long ago to an aversion to funerals. She'd assured him she'd be OK and understood. Yet here he was for her to lean on, albeit tight-faced, making sure she managed through what she considered to be the hardest thing she'd ever gone through.

Much harder than when her mother had left for whatever had appealed more than her young daughter. Much harder than several years back when she'd been notified the father she'd never known had died in a motor vehicle accident.

Losing Gramps was like losing a part of herself because he'd loved her, raised her, encouraged and nurtured her to be the woman she'd become. She'd loved him with her whole heart.

Now he was gone.

Time crawled as the funeral services concluded and the guests relocated to the graveside for a final farewell.

Weariness swept over Liz, tugging at her already exhausted body, but she kept her chin high and her shoulders straight as she paid her last respects to the grandfather she'd loved.

More tears pricked her eyes when she tossed the first handful of dirt onto the lowered casket. She turned, grateful to find Adam's broad shoulders waiting for her. She buried her face. His arms went around her, holding her close.

"Shh, sweetheart, he's in a better place."

She remained in his arms long enough to pull herself together, then wiped at her eyes. "I know."

Gramps was in a better place. Had to be. Those last few weeks he hadn't known who she was, had only registered that he couldn't breathe. He'd literally been drowning in his own body fluids, and no amount of diuretics had eased his suffering.

She sniffled, then received the line-up of graveside mourners. Gramps hadn't been social for years and had outlived most of his friends from younger days so most in attendance were her coworkers and friends. Adam's hand pressed into her lower back, providing the comfort she needed to accept each well-meant condolence, each heartfelt hug.

Her friend Kelly hovered close, keeping a watchful eye and offering her support repeatedly. A girl couldn't ask for a better friend, but at the moment Liz just wanted to curl into a lonely ball and cry at the loss of her grandfather.

By the time Adam assisted her into his luxurious two-seater, she practically dropped onto the plush seat. She couldn't recall ever feeling so drained mentally, emotionally, or physically, not even after pulling a double shift.

Now she'd go home to a house filled with reminders of Gramps, filled with a hospital bed in her living room because there hadn't been room for his bed and equipment in either of the two tiny bedrooms. Plus, she'd liked him being able to look out the windows at the small flower garden she kept well tended even if it meant getting up at the crack of dawn to do so.

Gramps had loved roses, said they reminded him of her grandmother. Even after he'd forgotten most everything, he'd lie in his bed and stare at the blooms outside the window for hours. Liz was pretty sure better times had filled his thoughts, times when his body and mind had been strong, and he'd been happy.

"You OK?" Adam asked before sliding his key into the ignition.

She took a deep breath. Time to start letting go, to

cherish her memories of her grandfather rather than aching over her loss. She could do this. "Just really tired."

Adam paused from reversing the car out of the parking place to look at her. Tension marred the handsome lines of his face. What did those all too intense eyes of his see?

"It's been a long couple of days," he finally said, easing the car out of the lot. "You've not slept enough to count."

True. She'd barely closed her eyes since the moment she'd tried to resuscitate Gramps and failed. Had it only been early Sunday morning?

"There'll be plenty of time for sleep now that Gramps is gone." She tried not to sniffle at the words. At the reality her life had become a whole lot less complicated three days ago. And very empty. Panic seized her chest, and she fought another wave of tears. "What am I going to do without him?"

"You'll get by." Adam shot her an empathetic look. "One day at a time. With each day that passes the pain will be a little more bearable. Life will go on, Liz. I promise."

One day at a time. In her head, she knew he was right, but her heart didn't want right. Her heart wanted her grandfather.

"I miss him already."

He nodded in understanding. "The house won't be the same without him."

"I wish you'd met him before he got so sick," she mused.

Adam was everything her grandfather admired in a man. Everything she admired in a man, for that matter. He'd been so good to her during Gramps's illness.

"He was such a joy." Her voice broke. "The best gramps who ever lived."

"Not that you're biased." His gaze softened, full of compassion, before returning to the road.

"Of course not," she agreed, smiling at him through her tears and counting her blessings that she had Adam to see her through this horrible time.

Adam hated seeing Liz so devastated, but they'd known for months this day would come. Actually, Gramps had held on much longer than he, Liz, or any of numerous doctors had ever thought possible.

Then again, Gramps had had a fabulous nurse who'd loved her grandfather very much and had refused to let him go. This last time she hadn't been able to pull off another medical miracle.

Personally, Adam thought Gramps had longed for the release death had offered his broken body and mind. He'd occasionally caught a pleading glimmer in the old man's eyes, a glimmer that begged Adam to convince Liz to let him go, to give her a reason to move on beyond trying to mend the unfixable.

Her red-rimmed eyes tore at his heart, making him long for the ability to ease her sorrows. As a doctor he dealt with death routinely. In many ways he'd hardened himself to bereavement, but seeing Liz so upset, so unlike her usual unflappable self, got to him. First hand, from losing his parents, he knew only time would chip away at the horrendous pain in her heart, but if possible he'd move heaven and earth to put the light back into her eyes.

Ignoring the zig-zag of pain at his right temple, he pulled onto the highway, heading toward town. The cemetery where Gramps had been buried next to Liz's grandmother was located about twenty miles outside the city limits. He wanted to get Liz home, feed her, and put her to bed. She looked ready to drop and the pain in his head refused to ease.

"The house is going to seem so quiet," she mused from where she sat in the passenger seat, staring out the window at cornfields filled with a bumper crop thanks to all the rain they'd had so far this Mississippi summer.

"I'll stay with you," he immediately offered. He'd stayed the previous two nights. The first, he'd sat with her on the tiny loveseat that served as the only sitting area in her crowded living room. He'd held her while she'd talked about Gramps, while she'd cried, while she'd napped for a few short hours just before dawn. Last night, he'd stayed on the sofa while forcing her to bed. He wasn't sure she'd slept any more than she had the previous night, but at least she'd made it to bed. Of course, when he'd awakened early this morning, she'd been curled next to him, eyeing Gramps's hospital bed.

She nodded. "I'd like that. I don't want to be by myself."

No way would he leave her to face tonight alone.

Then again, if she went back to her place, all Gramps's things were just as she'd left them, just as they'd been on the day the old man had died. Liz wouldn't sleep. She'd sit in the living room, staring at that empty hospital bed.

In testament to how troubled she was she didn't notice when he drove past the turn-off leading to the small frame house her grandfather had lived in for more than fifty years. Her hands rested in her lap and she looked ghostly pale.

"I'll stop and pick us up some take-out on the drive home. I've not seen you eat a bite."

She grimaced, shaking her head. "I don't think I can eat anything. I'm sure it's nerves, but the thought of food makes me want to throw up."

"You need to eat."

"I will, but not right now. I just want to lie down and close my eyes to reality for a while."

She'd barely nibbled at a few crackers yesterday. Less than that today. He didn't like her lack of appetite, but perhaps she was too exhausted to eat. He'd get some of the soup his cleaning lady had left him on her last visit and convince Liz to eat at least a little.

"Where are we?" she asked, pushing a strand of her dark hair away from her face and becoming aware that they'd long passed her street.

"I'm taking you to my place. You'll rest better."

"But I..." She paused. "You're right. I really don't want to face that empty hospital bed."

He'd known, just like he knew so much about the woman in the car with him. For the past year she'd been a constant part of his life.

That was a year longer than any other woman.

Since he'd had no intention of committing to anything beyond his career for many years to come, he hadn't thought it fair to become involved. Sure, he'd dated, but always with a clear understanding.

Liz had been different. She hadn't been looking for marriage and children either. She'd already been a hundred percent committed to caring for her grandfather and no relationship would change that.

She'd been safe.

Not that he'd meant to date her, to become part of a couple with her, but from the moment they'd met he and

Liz had hit it off. She was funny, intelligent, and sexy as hell. Without him realizing what had been happening, she had become more and more entrenched in his life until he couldn't imagine not having her smile brighten his day.

With Liz he'd found himself wanting marriage, children, all the things he'd once found superfluous to his medical career. Had she been free, he'd have begged her to walk down the aisle with him, to be his wife, the mother of his children.

But Liz's priority had been to her grandfather and he'd understood that. Understood and loved her all the more for her loyalty and big heart.

All the reasons hindering their relationship from moving forward had dissipated the moment Gramps had taken his last breath.

Another sharp pain cut through Adam's temple, momentarily blurring his vision and reminding him that perhaps not all the reasons were gone. A pain that had become more and more familiar over the past two weeks, as had the blurred vision.

So familiar that he'd seen a family physician friend of his to get a prescription for a headache medication on Friday.

Only his friend had been concerned his symptoms were more than just stress-induced. Particularly when upon being questioned Adam had admitted to feeling tired and having had muscle cramps recently. Larry had scheduled Adam for fasting bloodwork and a magnetic resonance imaging—MRI—scan of the brain on Monday. Only Adam had rescheduled the tests because of Gramps's death.

Surely Larry was being overly cautious?

But Adam couldn't suppress the niggle of fear that his friend was right. Something more was going on inside his body. Something bad.

Something that Adam wasn't sure he wanted to know.

Had he not been driving, he would have closed his eyes.

"What are you thinking?" Liz interrupted his thoughts, causing him to glance her way. She'd quit staring out the car window and watched him with her soulful brown eyes.

"Just hoping I left the place clean," he prevaricated. Now was not the time to tell Liz about the symptoms he'd been having. She already had enough to worry about.

"Mrs Evans keeps your condo immaculate and you're a neat freak of the worst kind, Adam." Her lips hinted at a smile. "I'd be highly shocked to find your underwear strewn around."

"That's because you visit after Mrs Evans has been there," he warned, pleased at the smile on her pale but beautiful face. Neither the dark circles ringing her eyes nor their red puffiness could hide Liz's beauty. She radiated from the inside with a natural exquisiteness he found irresistible.

Adam stared out at the road, squinted to clear his right eye of its haze. Unsuccessfully.

What if something bad was wrong with him?

He'd seen the concern on Larry's face and he hadn't even revealed his other symptoms to his friend.

Somehow saying out loud that his surgeon hands had gone numb for a few minutes last week, that at times pins and needles prickled his fingertips and that had been the real catalyst to his visit to Larry, seemed to make his symptoms all so much more real.

No, he hadn't admitted to anyone that his internal circuits had seemed to be going haywire from time to time over the past two weeks. Not even to himself.

CHAPTER TWO

ADAM stared at the shadowy living-room ceiling and listened to the soft chimes of the mantel clock that had once been his mother's.

One o'clock.

He owed it to his patients to get some sleep, but no matter how much his brain knew that, how many times he told himself to close his eyes, sleep remained elusive.

Probably because every fiber of his being was aware that while he was lying on his sofa with a cotton throw tossed over his body, Liz slept in his bed.

He'd planned to join her, but she'd been sound asleep. He hadn't wanted to risk going into his bedroom since any noise he inadvertently made might wake her. She needed to sleep. He'd never seen her look so worn out.

He'd changed out of his suit into a pair of shorts he'd pulled from the dryer, and hit the sofa. Maybe if he checked on Liz, knew she was OK, maybe then he could catch a few hours before going to the hospital.

Who wanted a doctor taking out their gallbladder or repairing their hernia when he hadn't slept much for three nights straight?

OK, so he hadn't been sleeping much for the past couple of weeks, which probably explained why he was having the episodes of blurred vision, fatigue, and paresthesia in his fingertips.

It was apparent he couldn't sleep until he knew Liz was OK. He'd sneak in, reassure himself, then he'd be able to get some shut-eye.

A few hours' rest and he'd be as good as new. A few hours sleep, and he'd probably be able to laugh away the fear he'd been squelching for days.

That did it. He was going to check on her. Just a quick peek.

He threw the cover to the opposite end of his sofa and padded barefooted to his bedroom door. The door was partially open where Liz had left it prior to the hot bath he'd forced her to take in the en suite. He crept into the room without having to open it wider.

The lamplight shone, illuminating her face. She lay half on her side with her arm draped over his pillow. Her chest rose and fell in even breaths. Her hair was tousled about her face. Her eyes were closed and, although he could tell she'd cried herself to sleep from the lingering puffiness, she looked to be sleeping peacefully at the moment.

There. He'd reassured himself she was OK. Now he could go to sleep. He crept toward the door.

"Adam?" Liz's sleepy voice stopped him.

He turned, met her heavy gaze. *He should have known better than to risk waking her.*

"Where are you going?" she asked, looking half-asleep with her sultry eyes and tousled hair. Her lips were parted, prettily plump. She looked beautiful, vulnerable.

"I didn't mean to wake you."

Realizing the lamplight still shone, she became more awake, glanced at the clock, and propped herself up on her elbows. "You're just now coming to bed?"

"I took the sofa."

"You're sleeping on the sofa?" Her forehead creased in confusion. "Why?"

"You need to sleep."

"I need you to hold me," she countered, her eyes dark and needy.

This was why he'd come in here. He hadn't needed to check on Liz. He'd known she was just fine, that she was asleep, because if she hadn't been she'd have come to find him. He'd hoped she'd awaken. Hoped she'd invite him into his bed.

Because he'd been the one needing.

Needing to hold her, feel her warm body next to his, to breathe in the fresh scent of her shampoo.

Because he needed Liz. Needed her to comfort him. To allay his fears regarding whatever was going on inside his body. But how could he tell her? He couldn't. Why worry her when there might not be a thing to worry about? Telling her at this point would only be cruel.

He'd keep hiding his symptoms from her until he knew what he was dealing with, could assure that he wasn't going to be a burden on a woman who'd already faced more than her fair share of burdens.

"Adam?" She flipped back the covers, indicating for him to lie down next to her. "Hold me."

Adam eyed the bed, eyed the woman wanting him to join her, the woman he cared more for than anything else in life. He needed to hold her, to feel the aliveness within him that being with Liz always gave him.

He crawled between the sheets, wrapped his arms around her, and kissed the top of her head. So perfect for him. So what he'd never believed in prior to meeting her.

"Adam?" His name held questions, as if she sensed his unease, but her sweet warmness thawed the cold fear gripping him and he relaxed.

"Go back to sleep, sweetheart."

Yawning, she laced her fingers with his and snuggled closer. "Goodnight, Adam."

It was now, he thought, closing his eyes and almost instantly falling asleep.

Adam ignored the fatigue clawing at his body and carefully removed another section of Beverly Gilley's left breast.

He placed the tissue in a specimen tray. The pathologist would check to see if the forty-two-year-old's breast cancer had spread outside the lump that weeks of radiation had shrunk to a more surgically manageable size.

Resisting the urge to shake his hands back and forth to ease the tingling sensation burning his fingertips, he finished removing her left breast tissue and began examining the left axillary nodes. He'd remove a few of those to send to pathology, too. All he'd have left was to clean up the surgical site to make reconstruction easier at a later date and to sew up the incisions he'd made. If his hands kept bothering him, he'd let the nurse sew up the incision. Although not his normal routine, doing so was a common enough practice that no one would think too much of it.

He'd yet to remove a single node when the anesthesiologist became alarmed.

"Her oxygen sats are dropping," the doctor said, increasing the amount of oxygen he was delivering and simultaneously checking placement of Beverly's mask. "Something's not right."

"Pulse is up," the nurse said at his side. "Blood pressure is slightly elevated. Is she going into shock?"

Squelching the voice in his head asking if he'd somehow done something wrong, if he'd missed something because of his distraction with his hands, Adam did a quick assessment of his patient. Erythematous welts began appearing on her skin.

"She's breaking out in a rash," he said. "DC the anesthesia. Stat. She's reacting to it." He turned to the nurse. "Give epinephrine subcutaneously stat and then add diphenhydramine to her IV line."

"Yes, sir," the nurse said, giving the injection seconds later.

Adam hoped no one noticed that he massaged his fingers through the rubber gloves. *What was wrong with him?*

His gaze met the nurse's. He feigned calm, reassuring himself that she'd think his hand motions were due to stress, worry over his patient. *He was worried about his patient.* "We'll finish once she's stable."

Adam stayed with his patient until her vitals settled down, and he felt confident he could proceed without fear Beverly was in greater danger than normal.

Two hours later he propped his head against the doctors' lounge wall. The cold concrete soothed the throb in his skull. He ran over everything with Beverly's mastectomy, trying to recall if he'd done anything out of line, anything that might have made a difference in her outcome. He hadn't. Sure, he was tired, his right eye blurred and his fingertips burned. But even if he'd been at his best, he couldn't have prevented Beverly from reacting to the anesthesia.

Fortunately, they had gotten her severe allergic reaction under control before the situation had become even more critical. Before he'd been forced to deliver bad news to Beverly's waiting family.

"You OK?" Dr Roger Bell asked from behind him.

Startled, he raised his head. He hadn't heard the orthopedic surgeon enter the lounge.

"I heard what happened this afternoon," his friend said. "Dr Krick told me if you hadn't realized what was happening so quickly you might have lost the woman. Good going, man."

Adam shrugged. He couldn't let go of the idea that he might have somehow been at fault. "It's my job to keep my patients safe."

Was he compromising his patients' safety just by operating on them? But he couldn't put his life on hold while he awaited test results. Tests he needed to re-schedule and have done so he could await results. Why was he procrastinating?

"But not your job to predict the future," Roger countered, pulling items from his personal locker. "No one can say when someone's going to have an unexpected allergy like that. Not even you."

Hearing his earlier thoughts from an excellent surgeon like Dr Bell reassured him that what happened with Beverly truly hadn't been his fault. Still, he couldn't quite shake his guilt.

"Just thought you should know that those in the OR with you this afternoon were impressed with how quickly you came up with the correct diagnosis and credit you with saving the woman's life. The nurses are saying you're brilliant." Dr Bell added the last with a grin.

Brilliant? He'd been tired, distracted, wrestling with his fingers, and hadn't been at his peak. Far from brilliant. "Like I said, I was just doing my job."

Dangling a shower bag and fresh clothes, Dr Bell closed his locker. "I was surprised to hear you were back today. I figured you'd take off a while with Liz. I was really sorry to hear about her grandfather."

Adam nodded at his colleague. "I'll let her know."

Roger lingered rather than hitting the showers. "You planning to make an honest woman of her now that she's free?"

None of your damn business, was what he wanted to growl, but instead he met his friend's eyes. "Liz and I have no definite plans for the future."

He couldn't make plans with Liz until after he'd had the tests Larry had ordered, until he knew what the hell was going on with him.

Until he knew if he had a future to plan.

"Your lab results all came back perfect," Larry, the family physician Adam had been good friends with since he'd moved to Robertsville, said. From the look on Larry's face, not everything had come back perfect, though.

"The MRI?"

Larry took a deep breath, met his gaze head on.

Premonition filled Adam. This was going to be bad. Very bad. Like maybe he didn't want to know after all bad.

"I wish I could say it was perfect, too, but it wasn't." Larry didn't seem in a hurry to tell Adam the results, seemed to be struggling with how to wrap his tongue around the words.

"Just get on with it," Adam spat out, no longer willing to wait patiently for the results of the scan he'd gone for yesterday morning.

Did he have a brain tumor? It was the explanation that kept running through his mind. Then he'd tell himself he was being foolish, a hypochondriac of the worst kind. Of course his scan was going to come back normal. Of course he was going to be just fine and have a future with Liz.

Brain tumors didn't happen to regular guys like himself. Not in the prime of their lives.

"Your MRI showed demyelization of gray matter in your brain."

Demyelization? The breakdown of the protective lining around nerve cells? But…

"What does that mean?" Even as he asked, possibilities ran through his mind. Demyelization. An autoimmune response. His body was attacking itself? Why the hell would it do that? Why now?

Larry took another breath. "It means I'm going to schedule you to see a neurologist in Jackson."

"A neurologist?"

Larry looked at him oddly. Adam imagined he did sound a bit odd, but Larry was talking about his body, his life, his future. Could he help it if he was asking questions that as a physician he should know the answers to? Questions he did know the answers to? A neurologist specialized in diseases of the brain and nervous system. Demyelization diseases such as…no, he wouldn't go there. Wouldn't think the worst.

"There's a specialist in Jackson. He's involved in multiple sclerosis research."

Damn it. He'd just decided not to go there. With Larry saying the words out loud, he couldn't help but go there.

"MS?" Did he sound as blown away as he felt? MS. He could end up paralyzed, completely dependent on others for even the most basic of things. He didn't have MS. He couldn't have MS.

"I want you to see Dr Winters. I put in a call to his office as soon as I got your report. He's out of town at a convention until next week, but you're scheduled for an early morning appointment on his first day back in the office."

"MS?" he repeated. There had to be a mistake. The MRI must be wrong. This wasn't happening to him.

"With the demyelization, I have to consider MS on the list of differential diagnoses. You know that. You'll need further testing before any diagnosis can be confirmed, but I suspect Dr Winters is going to verify my suspicion."

Adam winced, knowing what that further testing would involve. "A spinal tap."

Larry nodded. "And evoked potential testing, where an electrical impulse is applied to various parts of your body to see how the nerve cells conduct the impulse and if there's any demyelization of the peripheral nerve cells."

Adam attempted to digest what he was being told. MS. Him. It couldn't be true.

Visual changes. Pin-prickling sensations in his

fingers. Numbness in his hands. Fatigue. Muscle aches and weakness. Headaches.

Hell. It could be true.

If it was true, his entire life would never be the same.

If true, he would lose everything he'd ever held dear. His career. Liz.

Because there was no way in hell he'd ever tie Liz to a doomed man, and if he had MS that's exactly how he saw himself. Doomed.

CHAPTER THREE

FROM where Liz spoke to the director of the assisted living facility where she was donating Gramps's medical equipment, she glanced toward the man coming through the automatic glass door.

Despite the gloom of the occasion and her grief of the past week and a half, her heart lightened at seeing Adam. Her gaze met his blue one and she flashed a quick smile at him, but he looked distracted. Actually, he'd seemed distracted all morning.

Bless him, he'd been really busy in the OR ever since he'd run into complications with a breast cancer patient's mastectomy on the day after Gramps's funeral. He'd spent the night at the hospital in case the woman had problems during the night. Since then, they'd gone to dinner a few times, but he'd been distracted, his mind obviously on work.

Kind, dedicated, dependable, decent—all those words described the man carrying in Gramps's nearly new walker.

"Is there anything more?" she asked, feeling guilty that he'd had to finish by himself. She'd helped carry in the first load, but the medical director had stopped her to express gratitude for the equipment that would now be loaned out to those in need.

"I think this is the last of it except for the hospital bed," Adam said, placing the walker next to the other items he'd carried in. Beneath his T-shirt his muscles rippled and Liz sighed in appreciation of his physical beauty. No doubt about it, Adam was a gorgeous man, but his inner beauty was what had stolen her heart.

He'd borrowed a friend's truck and helped haul the equipment. Getting rid of the medical equipment, the signs of Gramps's prolonged illness, had seemed the easiest place to start in going through his things. Besides, she needed that hospital bed out of her living room or she was going to cry herself silly. Her grandfather would have wanted the equipment donated to some needy person who might otherwise have to do without.

Yes, giving away the equipment was a good beginning. She'd tackle Gramps's wardrobe and closet later, when she felt stronger, more capable of dealing with the emotional baggage that would come with doing so.

She glanced toward Adam and found him clutching the handles of Gramps's walker. White-knuckled, he wore a far-away look, as if he imagined being forced to use assistive devices for ambulation. Was he remembering the few times early in their relationship when Gramps had puttered along behind the walker he'd quickly grown too debilitated to use?

"I'll get a couple of male employees to assist you with the hospital bed," Glenda volunteered, interrupting Liz's heartfelt stare.

Whatever Adam's thoughts, he shook them off and nodded at the director. "Thanks."

Two maintenance workers helped guide the bed off the truck and they rolled it inside the building.

Liz bit the inside of her lip as she watched the bed being rolled down the hallway.

"It'll be alright," Adam said from beside her. She glanced toward him, his gaze fixed on the disappearing hospital bed. At first she'd thought he was reassuring her, but despite the fact he stood next to her, he didn't seem aware she was there. His attention riveted on that bed, not her.

In her grief she'd forgotten that during the time she and he had been dating, Adam had spent a lot of time with her grandfather. He'd loved Gramps, too.

Oh, Gramps.

"It seems strange," she said softly, placing her hand on Adam's arm. "That bed has been a central part of my life for so many months. When I think that I'll never see it again, I…" Her voice trailed off.

Adam's gaze cut to her. He took her hand and gave a gentle squeeze. "I know."

"Thank you," she whispered, standing on tiptoe to kiss his cheek. "Losing Gramps is the hardest thing I've ever dealt with. You've been so wonderful, Adam. I can't imagine not having you by my side."

An odd look passed over his face. One she almost thought laden with guilt. But that was ridiculous. Adam had nothing to be guilty about. Still, the look caused nervous tremors in her stomach.

"Oh, Liz! We're so happy with the equipment. Thank you. Thank you. Thank you," Glenda gushed, returning to their side. The woman sent an engaging smile toward Adam. "And, Dr Cline, it's always a pleasure to see you."

Liz thought so, but wasn't sure she liked the way Glenda eyed Adam's body. Still, she couldn't blame the woman for admiring what so deserved female admiration.

Adam in form-fitting but not too tight jeans and his black T-shirt was the kind of pin-up calendar fantasy women dreamed of meeting in real life.

"I know you aren't dressed for house calls…" Glenda swept her gaze over Adam again "…but Irene Guess has a wound I think is going to need debridement. About a year ago she had a similar wound she was hospitalized for. Would you mind taking a quick look so I'll know whether or not to schedule an appointment? It's so hard for her to get in and out, not to mention getting her a ride. I thought while you're here you might have a quick look."

Adam didn't bat an eyelid at being asked to check a patient during his day off. But Liz couldn't help but wonder if it bothered him because he rubbed his right temple. He caught her watching him and quickly dropped his hand.

Finding his behavior odd, Liz followed him and Glenda to check on Mrs Guess. The older woman was sitting on her sofa, watching a soap opera. She seemed more interested in the program than in discussing the wound the director was concerned about.

Adam washed his hands, massaging the soap into his fingertips for longer than normal, once again making Liz question if he felt OK. But with a smile on his face, he dried his hands before putting on gloves and assessing the older lady, asking about the sore that had come up on her abdomen.

"I don't know what caused it," Mrs Guess said in her sweet grandmotherly voice, her gaze still on the television. "I woke up with a red spot one morning, and each day it's worse than it was the day before."

"Does the area drain?"

The woman waited until a man on television finished expounding an argument in court to a serious-looking jury. Once the scene cut to a commercial, she shifted her glasses-rimmed eyes to Adam. "Yellowish stuff is on the bandage when I take it off."

"Can you show me the place while sitting, or do I need to help you lie down?"

"You can see." Mrs Guess raised her shirt and lifted a pasty white skin roll. A gauze pad crumpled. She removed the pad and held the bandage out. "This is the drainage I was talking about. Just yellowish gunk."

"I see." But Adam's gaze had already taken a quick glance at the dirty dressing and gone to the ulceration on the woman's abdomen. An open nickel-sized lesion with a large area of surrounding redness oozed a sticky honey-colored exudate. Streaks of angry red shot out.

Liz had seen worse wounds, but Mrs Guess did have a serious problem. From the look of the ulcer and drainage, she'd need IV antibiotics and possibly isolation as discovering MRSA had caused the infection wouldn't surprise her.

"Have you had a fever, Mrs Guess?"

"How am I supposed to know?" She seemed annoyed that Adam had asked her another question now that the program she'd been watching had come back on.

"I don't have a thermometer, but I have felt a tad warm the past day or two. I thought it was from the heat."

Adam took her hand, forcing her to keep her attention on him rather than the television. "You've got an infection. From the way the wound looks, I suspect a particular strand of Staph." He confirmed Liz's suspicions. After burning the gloves and washing his hands again, Adam returned to Mrs Guess's side. "I'm going to call for a non-emergency ambulance to take you to the hospital."

The woman looked alarmed. "The hospital? Surely a little sore isn't that serious?"

"It can be. You need strong antibiotics through an IV. In the morning I'll recheck you and may opt to surgically clean the wound. Similar to what I did last year to the place on your leg." Placing his fingertips to his temple, Adam closed his eyes and rubbed the spot for such a brief moment that someone who didn't know him so well might have missed the tell-tale action. Liz saw.

Did he have a headache? After he finished with Mrs Guess, she'd offer to drive the truck back to his place, run him a hot bath, maybe give him a neck rub. Goodness knew, he hadn't been getting enough rest with the hours he was pulling at the hospital. But he'd said he needed to make up for the couple of days he'd taken off to be with her following Gramps's death.

But when Adam turned to Liz, any traces of a problem had disappeared and he wore only a concerned professional expression. "I'll drop you by your place and meet the ambulance at the hospital. That way I can do a direct admission and Mrs Guess won't have to go through the emergency room."

"I'll go with you." She'd be there when he finished. She wanted to ask him about his headache, to make sure he got some rest tonight. He'd been taking such good care of her. Tonight she'd make him prop his feet up and she'd pamper him.

Not meeting her eyes, he shook his head. "No, I'll drop you at your place. I may be a while."

Huh? Liz blinked at him, sure she failed to hide her surprise. "I'd rather go with you."

"Liz," he began, and she'd swear he winced. "I need to make rounds on my other patients. It would be better to drop you off since I don't know how long I'll be."

She didn't bother to point out that until Glenda had asked him to check Mrs Guess he'd planned to spend the entire day with her. But she did think it and wondered why he'd want to drop her at her place.

They'd always had to make use of every available second because of busy schedules and her limited free time. Maybe he thought time wasn't so precious now that Gramps was gone and the confines of their relationship not so rigid.

Yet she'd barely seen him since the day of Gramps's funeral.

"I don't mind," she assured him, sending a smile his way to let him know she wanted to spend whatever time they could together. Later, when they were in private, she'd reassure him that every moment they spent together was precious.

"But I do," he stunned her by saying. He cast a quick glance at Glenda and Mrs Guess, then continued. "You've been clearing out your grandfather's things all day. The last thing you need is to get stuck at the hospital for hours on end. I'm taking you home."

Bewildered, Liz nodded her agreement, knowing there must be a good reason he didn't want her with him.

* * *

"Adam? Is something wrong?" Liz asked the following night. Concern filled her voice and he could just picture her twirling a strand of hair around her finger while she asked.

Adam closed his eyes and gripped his cellular phone all the tighter.

From his caller ID he'd known the caller was Liz. So why had he answered? He should have just avoided the call altogether.

Avoiding Liz was what he'd done for the past twenty-four hours. Why stop now?

But he'd eventually have to talk to her, tell her that he was…was what? No longer a whole man? Not healthy? Not sure exactly what was going on with his body, but that he'd be seeing the neurologist for a spinal tap and the other tests in the morning?

On Monday the specialist had agreed with Larry. He believed Adam had MS.

Which was why he'd wanted to spend yesterday with Liz, but gripping that walker in his palms had messed with his head, had panicked him. All he'd been able to think was that if he had MS, the day might come when he wouldn't be able to walk without a walker. Or worse. The day might come when he wouldn't be able to walk at all.

Each time he'd looked at Liz, all he stood to lose had constricted his throat, made it difficult to breathe, made him afraid she'd see the anxiety in his eyes.

Then, while examining Mrs Guess, a searing pain had stabbed the right side of his head, making him wonder if he'd black out from the intensity.

Even in her distress over losing her grandfather, Liz was too smart to miss that something was wrong with him. She'd noticed yesterday. He couldn't keep hiding his symptoms from her. Others perhaps, but not Liz. She knew him too well.

He should have told her the moment he'd started having the blurred vision, the pinpricks in his fingers, the tiredness. He should have told her the night her grandfather had died. Before then.

Instead, he'd pretended that everything was fine, not letting on that he was having symptoms of any kind.

He'd thought he was saving her pain by delaying, but the more time that went by the more he wondered if he wasn't making things more difficult by keeping his symptoms, his fears to himself.

He should tell her now.

He opened his mouth, intent on telling her the truth. "I'm just busy."

That wasn't what he'd meant to say. Not even close.

"OK." She didn't sound convinced. He didn't blame her. His unusual behavior confused her. Hell, he was pretty confused himself.

Silence buzzed over the line, acutely broadcasting that change was eminent whether he wanted it or not.

"I looked for you after I finished my shift. They told me you'd already left for the day. Are you coming over? I could order take-out." Her voice held hopefulness.

"Not tonight," he managed to say. What if he had another episode of pain? How would he explain it to her? "I had a long day and am tired." True. He seemed to always be tired these days. "I'm flying to Alpharetta in the morning and want an early start."

A lame excuse and they both knew it. An avid pilot of his own Cessna, a scheduled trip had never stopped him in the past. And why had he lied to her? He was going to Jackson, to see the specialist, to find out the truth behind his symptoms.

Which was why he'd lied to her.

He didn't want her to worry, didn't want her sympathy, didn't want her to possibly be tied to another invalid. Liz deserved a life.

"If you're sure, then…" She hesitated, making him want to tell her how much he needed her, just to have her wrap her arms around him and tell him everything would be OK, that she'd be there for him no matter what those damned tests showed.

The crux of it was Liz would be there for him in a heartbeat. If he let her. But he wanted better than that for her. Lots better.

Be strong, man. You've got to see this through, find out for sure what's going on before involving Liz.

"Sorry, Liz, but I've got to go." He hung up before she could say anything more.

But mostly before he could say anything more.

The next morning Adam sat in a Jackson Neurology Clinic exam room, staring at a framed Norman Rockwell print that hung on the wall opposite him.

Too bad real life wasn't as idyllic as Norman Rockwell presented it.

When the neurologist walked into the room, Adam knew by the expression Dr Winters wore that the test results hadn't been good.

By now he should be used to that expression. Hadn't every bit of news he'd gotten thus far been bad?

The neurologist pulled up his stool, glanced down at

the piece of paper containing words that would forever change Adam's life, and then glanced up. "There's no good way to put this and we pretty much already knew what the conclusions of the tests were going to be, so I'm going to be blunt. You have MS."

Adam's ears roared. His blood boiled. His skin crawled. He gritted his teeth. He clenched his tingling fingers. Still his body threatened to explode from the impact of those words.

He had MS.

"You're sure?"

"Yes. The analysis of the cerebral spinal fluid shows protein, cells, and increased antibody production. Antibodies containing oglioclonal bands. Unfortunately, that in combination with the demyelization revealed on the MRI are conclusive even if the evoked potential testing hadn't been positive."

There was that damned expression again.

"But they were positive, too, weren't they?" Because all his tests pointed in one direction. A direction he didn't want to go, but had no choice but to take.

He had MS.

The specialist nodded. "I'm sorry."

All night he'd lain in bed preparing himself for this, preparing to hear that his body was attacking itself. Yet he shook. Any moment he expected the earth to open, for lightning to strike, for a tornado to rip him from the ground. Because any of those things were possible and expected in this horrible nightmare.

This had to be a nightmare.

God, he hoped it was only a nightmare.

He couldn't have a debilitating disease. Not him. Not when he had so much to live for. So much he wanted to do with and give to Liz.

MS.

He shuddered. His stomach churned. His heart sank. Fate couldn't be this cruel.

Could it?

He closed his eyes and forced himself together. Forced his emotions under control. Well, not control, but the closest he could manage. He doubted he'd ever feel in control of his body, *his life*, again.

Steeling himself for the worst, he met the specialist's gaze. "What does this mean, exactly? What should I expect?"

Did he even want to know? With the way things had gone thus far, perhaps he shouldn't ask. Perhaps ignorance was bliss. Before seeing Larry, he'd known something was wrong but hadn't felt this heavy sense of impending doom.

"Since this is your first known exacerbation, it's difficult to say. As you probably already know, symptoms vary from individual to individual just as the course of the disease varies. It's possible this exacerbation could go away tomorrow and you won't have another episode for decades." Dr Winters shrugged. "Maybe never."

"It's also possible that this is only the tip of the iceberg, that what I'm experiencing is mild and will get much worse before going into remission—if I go into remission at all."

"That's true. There's no way of knowing the course of your individual disease, or how progressive your case will be," Dr Winters agreed. "Generally there are considered to be four classifications of MS, each a different level of progression of the disease."

"There's no way to know which type I have, is there? No test or study that can be done to determine which one?"

"With time we'll know, but as far as a test I can run..." the doctor shook his head "...there's not. The best we can hope for is that this will be your only exacerbation and that you've already experienced the worst of your symptoms."

"But that's not what you expect?"

Dr Winters frowned. "You know I can't predict the future. Anything I said would only be a guess."

"I could lose control of my body functions, go paralyzed, even die from this."

"That type of progression is rare, Adam. The majority of MS cases fall into the category where the person only has a few exacerbations throughout his or her lifetime." Dr Winters gave a stern look. "You can't go into this thinking the worst. You have to fight, keep a positive outlook."

But no matter how Adam tried to focus on the positive, on the fact that this might go away, the stark reality wouldn't let up.

"I could end up in a wheelchair. Crippled." He winced. "Bedridden."

Just like Gramps.

The thought of Liz putting her life on hold to wait on him hand and foot while he lay in a hospital bed caused bile to rise up his throat.

"What about my job? My career? I'm a surgeon with MS." He laughed with ill humor.

He felt like he'd made an admission much as an alcoholic would at an AA meeting. Hi, my name is Dr Adam Cline, and I'm a surgeon with MS. Only with alcoholism a person could fight. How did one fight one's own haywire immune system?

"Am I medically clear to perform surgeries? To pilot my plane?"

"For now," the neurologist said. "As long as you're physically and mentally capable. However, you should check with your airport on any regulatory guidelines that would restrict you from flying. But if your symptoms worsen, I'd have no choice but to put you on medical leave."

Adam liked his life. He had a great job, a hobby he loved, financial freedom, and Liz. Now all the best parts were slipping through his fingers like loose grains of sand. He wanted to grasp each bit, hold it all in place, but doing so was futile.

"Adam?" Dr Winters touched his forearm. "I'm concerned about you. You're not suicidal?"

His life might be over in many ways, but he wasn't a murderer and in his eyes suicide was a form of murder. He laughed with a bitterness he wasn't sure had ever come from his lips before. "Suicidal? No, I'm not suicidal."

Although he'd rather die than burden Liz with taking care of him for years on end.

"You know…" Dr Winters studied him "…there are lots of people who have MS who live fairly normal lives."

Adam nodded. There were, but he had to face facts. His life would never be the same. He had MS and no way of knowing that the future wouldn't leave him an encumbrance.

How could he do that to Liz? How could he put her in the position of having to take care of him that way? It would be like starting all over with her grandfather. Each day Liz would have to care for him, wonder if he'd be able to do anything for himself, if he'd know who she was, as memory issues occasionally went along with MS.

She'd lose all possibility of having a normal life.

They had to end. Continuing their relationship was condemning Liz to a life sentence.

He wouldn't be able to tell her why. She'd never let him walk away if she knew about his MS. Not his Liz. No, she'd insist on staying by his side, caring for him despite him trying to push her away so she wouldn't carry this burden.

He didn't expect her to understand. Not at first, but in the long run she'd discover he'd done the right thing to set her free.

What woman who'd already given up so much of her life to care for an invalid would want to take on that burden a second time?

Worse, what kind of man would he be if he knowingly let her?

CHAPTER FOUR

WHILE chatting on the phone with Kelly, Liz chopped a tomato. Her stomach protested at the thought of yet another salad, but she had to eat and these days her stomach protested at everything anyway. Tonight would be no exception regardless of what she ate so she'd at least eat healthily.

"I've barely seen Adam since my grandfather died. I miss him so much. We haven't spent enough time together for me to figure it out, but I know something is going on with him. He says nothing's wrong, but he's just not been himself."

"He has seemed a bit distracted at work lately," Kelly agreed, pausing in thought before saying, "Maybe he doesn't know what to say to comfort you and that makes him feel inadequate."

"Maybe." What Kelly said sort of made sense, but Liz wasn't convinced. Adam wasn't an inadequate kind of man. With reason. There wasn't a thing inadequate about Dr Adam Cline. Except his communication skills for the past month. "But Adam was perfect during Gramps's funeral and right afterwards. He held me and with his arms around me I knew everything would be all right. Just his being with me was enough."

She sighed. Kelly had to be tired of listening to her go on and on about Adam.

"Sorry, Kel. I know I've turned into a major whiner, but worrying about Adam is driving me crazy. I can't stand not seeing him or talking to him when it's so obvious something's bothering him. When I know he's not telling me something."

"If it was anyone other than Adam I'd ask if you thought he was seeing someone else."

With the way he hadn't been able to get rid of her fast enough on the day they'd gone to the nursing home and then so obviously avoiding her since then, that thought had crossed her mind, but she'd quickly dismissed it. Adam loved her and was the most honorable man she knew. If he was interested in someone else, he'd tell her.

"I don't understand what's going on with him, but I don't think it's another woman."

"Then you need to confront him. Make him tell you what's bothering him," Kelly advised, not for the first time. "Sorry to cut you short, but Jason's here." Kelly had dinner plans with the hospital pharmacist she had been dating on and off for the past few months. "I just called to check on you and to see if you'd had a chance to talk with Adam. I really think this is all just a misunderstanding of some kind. I'm sure he's fine. That everything's fine."

Guilt washed over Liz. Her friend had called to check on her and all she'd done had been to moan and groan.

"I'm sorry to lay all this on you." Eyeing the tomato wedges, she set the knife on the counter. "I'll talk to you tomorrow."

"Liz…" Kelly hesitated. "Promise me you'll get some rest and not let this keep eating away at you. You've lost weight and look so tired. I know you keep saying you're worried about Adam, but I'm worried about you."

"I'll try to get some rest." She would try. Not that that meant she'd actually get any sleep.

More often than not she caught herself lying in bed remembering the happy days before Gramps had got sick. Remembering him taking her down to Tillman's Hollow to go fishing in Riley Arnold's pond when she'd been a small girl. Remembering his laughter at Barney Fife's antics as they'd watched *The Andy Griffith Show*— Gramps's favorite. Remembering his look of pride when she'd graduated from high school with honors.

Tears welled in her eyes. No matter how many times she reminded herself that he was gone, when she dozed off she forgot and when she woke up again, fresh loss washed over her.

Just as fresh loss washed over her each time she remembered the reality that something was horribly wrong between her and Adam.

Why was he shutting her out?

Kelly was right. She needed to confront him, to talk with him and tell him how she felt.

She poured a glass of milk to drink with her salad and gathered her things to go to the living room. She set her plate on the antiquated coffee-table with its peeling veneer and plopped down on the worn, almost thread-bare love seat. Curling into the permanently indented furniture, she tucked her feet beneath her. But when she was comfortable, she didn't pick up her salad. Instead, she looked around the barren living room.

The whole house was barren. Empty. The only living part of the place was the roses that still bloomed brightly in the front yard. Roses that she could see if she flipped on the outdoor lights, but she hadn't done so since her grandfather had died.

Was Kelly right? Was Adam not dealing well with her grandfather's death and felt lacking in some way? Was he inadvertently pushing her away without realizing what he was doing?

But what about him rubbing his temple? Adam didn't have headaches. At least, she couldn't recall him ever having had one. Was it stress?

An insistent rap at her front door had her jumping up from the love seat. Her fork clanged against the plate, then onto the faded hardwood floor.

With Kelly on a date, only one person would show up at her door this late in the evening.

Excitement shimmied up her spine. Adam. He'd come to her. Finally. They'd talk, work through whatever had been bothering him.

On her way to the door she paused to stare at herself in the small framed mirror that hung on the wall.

Her hair remained pulled up in a loose ponytail, her face was clean-scrubbed, and she wore shorts and a T-shirt. But it was the dark circles and puffiness around her eyes that stood out most. She looked haggard even to her own eyes.

Maybe that explained Adam's recent avoidance.

Or maybe if she'd quit procrastinating and open the door, she'd know exactly what the problem was.

"Who's there?" she asked, her hand hesitating on the safety chain until she'd verified who was at the door.

"Adam."

Barely able to contain her happiness, she undid the chain and lock and stared in horror at the man who'd become so entangled with her very being.

He looked awful.

Even more so than she did. His hair was ruffled from him having repeatedly run his fingers through it. His face was pale, gaunt. And his eyes. Never had she seen such lost blue chasms indenting his face. Deep blue orbs that threatened to drown anyone who looked too closely.

"Adam? What's happened?" She reached for him, stopping short when he jerked back before her fingers made contact. As if he feared her touch.

"Adam?" she asked, uncertain how to take his reaction.

His gaze shot beyond her, never connecting with her face.

That's when she got a whiff of him. Still wonderfully masculine Adam. Spicy, musky, sexy, intoxicating to her senses, but something more. Something intoxicating in a very different way. A way very unlike Adam.

He'd been drinking, and not just the glass of wine they occasionally shared.

She stared at him, wondering if he was drunk.

At least that would explain his strange behavior.

Liz's anxiety increased tenfold. What was going on?

"Adam, has something bad happened?" She lifted her hand to touch him, almost crying out when he grimaced. "Tell me what's wrong. Please, Adam. I know something is wrong. Tell me."

Oh, Adam.

"Invite me in," he ground out in a voice she barely recognized as his. A voice that bordered on angry, cold, devoid of any feelings for her. "There is something I have to tell you, and I'd rather not do so standing in your doorway smelling these damned roses."

Liz's heart sank. Something bad had happened.

Or was about to happen.

Was Adam breaking up with her?

Had she been wrong in her confidence in their love?

All the feelings of the past, feelings of those who loved her walking away, slammed full force into her, usurping her belief in her ability to be loved.

No, she reminded herself, *Gramps loved you. You are lovable.*

But still childhood wounds opened. Her confidence wavered and she couldn't meet Adam's eyes.

"Come in," she said, and spun away, fighting tears.

She walked over to the sofa where she'd been sitting and picked up her plate. She really had no appetite, but needed her hands busy so she forked up a bite. Forced her mouth around the tasteless food.

He stood, watching her eat, making swallowing seem impossible beneath his stare.

"Good to see you're eating. You've lost weight and look awful."

What? She lifted her gaze to glare. "You come into my house and criticize me?" She couldn't help the defensiveness in her voice. Kelly had told her pretty much the same thing only minutes before, but that was her friend who hadn't been shunning her. Not someone who had been giving her the cold shoulder and winced when she'd reached for him.

"Stating the obvious isn't criticizing," he said matter-of-factly.

She dropped her gaze back to her plate, staring at a crouton, wishing he'd sit down so he wouldn't tower over her, wishing she understood what was going on, afraid of what that understanding might bring with it.

She closed her eyes, hoping all the warning bells sounding in her head were wrong.

"The past few weeks have been strained."

He had no idea.

"You've avoided me," she accused softly, struggling to keep her earlier defensiveness from slipping back into her voice. "I don't understand what's going on between us, Adam. If I've done something, just tell me. We'll discuss it and figure out how to make it right." She gulped. "If you don't want to make it right, well, we'll figure that out, too. Just tell me what's going on so I can understand."

His frustration became a palpable pulse between them. Without looking, she knew he raked his fingers through his hair. It's what he did when searching that genius mind of his for a solution to a problem.

Unfortunately, she was the problem.

Although she wanted to hang onto her faith in his feelings for her like a protective shield, she felt loss prickling at her soul, robbing her strength to hold herself together.

No. No. No. She would not cry. She wouldn't.

"Liz, I… You…" His voice broke, as if he was struggling as much as she was. As if he battled within himself and didn't know how to deal with whatever ailed him.

She glanced up, needing to see what was on his face, in his heart, because for the life of her she just didn't understand what was happening between them.

He'd jerked away from her touch.

"Aw, Liz, I can't do what I came to do." With those strangled words he took her hands, pulled her to her feet and into his arms. "Lord, forgive me," he whispered into her hair, "but I just can't."

Can't what? she wondered, meant to ask, but he held her tight, closed his eyes and nuzzled her neck, inhaling her scent. Held her like he'd missed her every bit as much as she'd missed him, maybe more.

"Liz," he moaned. "My sweet, beautiful Liz."

His lips covered hers. Not a slow and tender kiss, but the kiss of a desperate man, a man who wanted her and couldn't go one more moment without kissing her. A man who needed her.

Her brain warned that she should stop him, that things weren't right between them. That something terrible had been going on for the past few weeks. That she'd gotten the impression he'd come to break off their relationship.

She knew all those things, but she couldn't stop Adam any more than she could stop the sun from rising. Not when he was so clearly tormented, when he so clearly did need her.

She melted against the man she loved.

She wrapped her arms around his neck, her fingers tangled in his hair, and she moaned as he pressed her tightly to him. His big hands caressed her back, molded her hips, cupped her buttocks in gentle but insistent motions.

He touched her, caressed her, kissed her, whispered sweet words of endearment to her.

This was insane. Her pride urged her to take heed, to

stop and demand where he got his nerve to be on the verge of breaking her heart one moment and making love to her the next. But pride was a poor friend, a poor lover, poor company, period.

Still, pride was all she really had these days.

That thought was strong enough to cause her to twist her mouth free just as his hands slid beneath her T-shirt. "Not like this. Not when I don't understand. Tell me, Adam. Tell me what's going on. What's happening between us."

"Liz." He leaned in, rained lingering kisses against her, oh, so receptive nape. Moist heat tickled the delicate skin, sending shivers over her body. His hands shimmied up her ribcage, his touch reverent. "Don't ask me questions I can't answer. Not tonight."

His fingertips skirted along the lower fullness of her bare-beneath-her-T-shirt breasts. Her breath caught, depriving her of oxygen as her body waged war with her mind.

"If you tell me what's going on, maybe I can help, Adam. Trust me."

"Just let me love you. Please," he coaxed in a husky tone.

More kisses along her neck, more urgent ones, more seductive ones. More brushes of his fingers until he palmed her breast in his hand and groaned his pleasure, made her moan with hers.

Too many weeks had gone by since they'd last made love. Too many lonely nights had passed. This, what they shared, the magic that passed between them when they touched, to her was an expression of what was inside, of what they felt for each other.

They shared a connection that transcended all else. Her pride. Her grandfather's death. His inability to deal with whatever was bothering him so much that he was pushing her away. They shared love.

Maybe that's what Adam needed. For her to love him. For her to give him all the love in her heart.

She would. They'd make love, talk, laugh at the silly insecurities she'd been dealing with, at how emotionally raw she'd felt. Adam would tell her how wrong she was, that his heart belonged to her and her alone. That this past month had been an aberration on his part and he'd been a fool, that nothing was wrong between them.

When a person wanted to believe desperately enough, she could convince herself of most anything.

Liz wanted to believe in Adam. She wanted to believe so much that she ignored all reason and clung to the hope she wasn't being naïve.

And if she was? She loved this man, felt his need, not just his physical need but his inner need to be loved, the need for the emotional bond they shared that meant they could face anything together. If she was naïve? So what? She would never turn her back on him when something so obviously ate at him, when he turned to her for comfort. She'd comfort with any means at her disposal no matter what the cost to herself.

She arched into his caresses, molded her lower body against his hips just as his tongue laved her nipple.

Tingles of awareness shot through her. Awareness of Adam's hands, his lips, his hard body ground tightly against hers.

"I love you, Adam," she whispered against his lips when they returned to her mouth. "Whatever's wrong, know that I love you, that I'm here for you and want to help."

For a moment she thought she'd said the wrong thing, that he was going to pull away from her, but a dam burst within him and fire burned within his eyes.

"This is wrong." He gave her a desperate kiss. "But I need you so damn much, Liz."

She'd known he needed her. The fact he was admitting to his need shocked her, amazed her. Adam wasn't one to verbalize needs. Yes, she saw it in his eyes, recognized the all-consuming desire, but to hear him admit he needed her wound her stomach into knots, reinforced her desire to give him her all.

Adam needed her. Somehow, no matter what was going on with him, everything would work out. Because they had love on their side.

"Adam." She kissed him back, daring him to deny loving her when the smoldering light in his eyes said he did. "Love me, Adam."

Adam held Liz close, listening to the sounds of her even breathing, caressing a soft strand of her hair, soaking in her warmth and goodness.

Damn his weakness.

He'd come to set her free, but he ached inside. Ached from his doctor's visit that morning, learning he really did have MS. Ached that in the blink of an eye he could lose his license to practice medicine, his license to fly a plane, his ability to be a man, his right to have this woman's love.

He ached for the loss of hope. He'd never be free to accept Liz's love, never be able to offer her a future, to give her a happily-ever-after.

Perhaps on this day when he'd first learned of the definite diagnosis of his disease, he was self-pitying. Perhaps in the morning light the future wouldn't loom so gray. But at the moment he mourned the loss of his health, his hopes for the future, his right to a life with Liz.

He hadn't lied to her when he'd said he needed her. He did need her. He needed the healing only her touch provided. Needed to feel her arms around him, needed to hear her sweet lips saying she loved him. Needed the peace she so freely gave him so he could figure out how he was going to face the future. A future that loomed bleakly ahead like a black hole greedily consuming everything good.

Even if just for one more night, he'd wanted to hold Liz, to be inside her, to feel her pleasure around him, to look into her eyes and see her world exploding within, and know that for the time they'd shared together his life had been good.

Yes, he was weak.

Yes, it was wrong.

But he faced an eternity of hellish loneliness.

Just the last few weeks' taste of not being with Liz scraped his insides raw. He'd gotten so accustomed to sharing the ups and downs of his day, of sharing laughter and sadness and even the quiet moments. When shared with Liz, every instant took on meaning.

This very moment held dear meaning, held his last taste of her sweetness, his last caress of her body, his last everything.

Although it would be all too easy to find himself cursing his diseased body, he wouldn't allow the self-pity to take over his mind, to cause him to weep in her arms. Instead he'd focus on everything good, focus on Liz, and the blessing she'd been in his life.

Making love to Liz was for him, not her, and he felt very guilty.

Sure, she'd looked content when she'd dozed off snuggled in his arms. Even now, in her sleep a satisfied smile played on her lips.

But he was a selfish jerk for being here. For clinging to something that could no longer be.

One night, he'd told himself when he'd foolishly taken her into his arms.

He'd had his night, and what a night it had been, but sunrise was only a few short hours away. He'd go before Liz woke up, go before the sun rose, but until the harsh reality of dawn came he'd hold her, breathe in her freshness, and cherish every second of what he feared would be the shortest but most precious few hours of his life.

Sparkly sunlight danced across Liz's face, but she didn't open her heavy eyelids. Her body felt deliciously warm inside, which seemed odd as she ached from the night's activities. The night's multiple activities.

Adam had been insatiable. A veritable tiger in bed. Lord, but she felt ravaged.

Thoroughly loved.

Smiling, she rolled onto her side, expecting to bump into his long, lean body.

She didn't.

That's when the quietness registered. No sounds of Adam breathing. No sensation of him being next to her.

Opening her eyes, only the imprint of where he'd slept remained in her bed. That and his spicy male scent.

A moment of panic raced through her, then she chided herself for her fear. He was probably in the bathroom. Or the living room. Or…he might have left.

She had to know.

Slipping out of the bed, she quickly discovered Adam wasn't anywhere in the small house.

She dropped onto the sofa, her nose twitching at her barely touched salad from the night before. A tiny gnat landed on a wilted leaf, giving testament to the sad state of her morning.

Adam had left without waking her.

Clammy heat covered Liz's body and she dry-heaved until her body ached.

CHAPTER FIVE

"*BUENAS dias, Señora Sanchez*," Liz greeted the recovering gallbladder patient in room twelve. She gave the woman a bright smile and explained that she'd be assessing her every hour.

Liz went through the routine vitals and was pleased to find the drowsy Hispanic woman's temperature, blood pressure, pulse, and respirations normal. She checked the three tiny surgical incision sites on her right upper quadrant.

"Everything looks wonderful," she explained in Spanish. Although not fluent, she had taken enough courses and listened to enough tapes while sitting with Gramps that she usually communicated without too many problems.

She made proper notations in the chart and explained that if everything remained well, Dr Cline would be by soon to write discharge orders. Surgery in the morning, home in the afternoon. Thank you, HMOs.

Adam. No, she wasn't going to think about him right now. It had been two days since he'd left her sleeping. She'd wanted to call him, to demand to know what was going on, but she hadn't.

Neither had he called her.

After making sure her patient was comfortable, Liz poked her head into May Probst's room. "How are you doing, May? Is there anything I can get for you?"

May hadn't been assigned to her this morning, but Liz knew the pleasant older woman well. She'd been a friend of her grandparents and often volunteered at the hospital through the women's auxillary. May had likely been the only true friend of Gramps to attend his funeral.

Unfortunately May had been having nausea for months that she'd written off as a peptic ulcer despite antacids only giving minimal relief. A few weeks ago she'd begun having stomach pain. Her abdominal CT had shown a questionable mass and Dr Mills, a young general surgeon whose father ran the hospital board with an iron fist, had performed exploratory laparoscopy that morning. Liz didn't like the arrogant young surgeon, but perhaps that was because he'd taken an instant dislike to Adam. Liz suspected it was a top-dog kind of thing. Dr Mills had a long way to go before he'd be the same caliber surgeon as Adam.

Cautiously scooting up in her bed, May gave a kind smile. "Kelly's taking good care of me so I can't complain."

"Can't? Or won't?" Liz moved to beside the bed and automatically raised the safety rail. "How did your procedure go? I've been swamped this morning and haven't had a chance to ask anyone."

May clasped her hands in her lap. "Dr Mills found my problem."

"I'm glad." But May's eyes held an odd light. "What exactly did he find?"

"The radiologist who read my CT scan was right. I do have a tumor."

Was May purposely being vague?

"Dr Mills removed it?"

"No," she softly denied. Too softly.

"No?" Liz asked. Something must have gone wrong for the surgeon not to have taken out the tumor. Generally, while the patient was already under anesthesia and on the operating table, the mass would have been excised. "Why not?"

May hesitated a few moments before lifting brave eyes to Liz. "Apparently, it's wrapped around my colon, ureter, renal artery, and perhaps my abdominal aorta."

"Oh, May." Liz covered her mouth with her hand. "I'm so sorry."

"Don't be sorry, child. It's not your fault."

"Dr Mills is going to schedule excision soon?"

Removing such a mass would be difficult, risky. Perhaps prior to proceeding the surgeon planned to consult with a vascular surgeon, perhaps a nephrologist, too.

May shook her head. "He says it's inoperable. That I'd die on the table and leaving it alone is my best option." She smoothed the crisp white sheet covering her. She wore a brave expression, but Liz didn't buy it.

"Your best option?" Liz scowled. "Is the tumor so slow growing that he doesn't think it'll kill you?"

May winced and Liz regretted her blunt statement. "I'm sorry, May. Sometimes I just want more aggressive treatments than those doctors deem the best option. I think you should get a second opinion by a more experienced surgeon."

May nodded. "That's OK. John wants a second opinion, too."

"Good. Get a second opinion. A third one, too, if necessary. I'm biased, but Dr Cline is an excellent surgeon." Excellent at breaking hearts, too, but May didn't need to know that. No matter what happened between her and Adam, he was by far the best surgeon in the area. "Perhaps you can schedule an appointment and let him look over your CT and Dr Mills's notes."

May nodded. "Dr Cline was my first choice, but he rescheduled my appointment first due to your grandfather and then again due to something personal. John didn't want me to wait another week and I ended up seeing Dr Mills."

Liz tried to hide her surprise. Adam had rescheduled appointments beyond the days he'd taken off with her following Gramps's death? Why would he do that? Where had he gone? What had he done?

Who was he with?

"John wants me to go to a larger hospital," May continued, oblivious to the turmoil rocketing through Liz. "One in Jackson."

Liz doubted Jackson held a finer surgeon than Adam, but refrained from saying so. The thought of him rescheduling patients had her mind spinning.

"Just you get that second opinion," she said firmly in an effort to hide her dismay.

"Enough about me." The older woman waved her hand dismissively, as if her problems were no big deal. "How are you holding up?"

Maybe she hadn't hidden her dismay so well.

For the briefest of moments Liz thought May was asking about the gaping hole in her chest, but no one knew about that. Fortunately Kelly had been spending quite a bit of time with Jason. Liz hadn't seen her friend until that morning, by which time she'd sort of pulled herself together and hadn't had to explain why her heart was so tattered. Kelly had asked, but they'd been interrupted and Liz hadn't been forced to go into any details.

Until May's revelation about Adam rescheduling appointments, she'd done a good job holding her act together.

May asked about her grandfather, though.

"As well as can be expected, I suppose." Considering everything. "I miss Gramps, but am trying to remember the good times we shared and move on with my life."

True. Regardless of what was going on with Adam, Liz would move forward with her life. For years she'd put her grandfather first, had planned to put Adam first for the rest of her life, but if he didn't want her love, she'd still find happiness. Perhaps she'd travel, see a bit of the world as a traveling nurse.

May looked pleased. "It's what he'd have wanted."

"Yes." Gramps had wanted great things for her. Great things like Adam.

She bit the inside of her lip and forced her thoughts elsewhere.

She chatted with May for a few more minutes, made sure she was comfortable, then went to check on her own patients.

Liz was pleased to find them all recovering as expected without complications. Two of her five patients were Adam's, which meant she'd have to see him.

Her stomach lurched at the thought. God, she wished whatever was going on with her stomach would pass.

She'd taken a handful of antacids yesterday and had obtained a little relief, but this morning her nausea had been right back. Truthfully, her stomach hadn't been right since Gramps's funeral. No wonder. She missed him so much. And then all this with Adam.

Stress definitely took its toll on a person's body but hopefully her nausea would soon pass and her appetite would return.

Recalling May, she decided that if her symptoms persisted much longer she'd have to see a doctor just to get reassurance.

"Everything OK with your patients?" Kelly asked when Liz arrived at the nurses' station. Her friend eyed her with worry.

"All's well at the moment."

Both nurses knew how quickly that could change.

Kelly punched her personal code into the medicine cart that tracked each nurse opening the medicine dispensing device. "I'm going to administer this, and then you're going to tell me what you have planned for this weekend. Jason's having a cookout and I want you to come if you aren't busy."

This weekend? Liz racked her brain, trying to recall what was going on the upcoming weekend. The fourth of July. She'd be working a twelve-hour shift on Saturday and Sunday.

The previous year's Fourth of July celebration sprang into her mind. She closed her eyes, picturing Adam and herself sitting on a blanket in the city park. They'd been holding hands, staring up at the bright, exploding lights in the sky. Adam had leaned in, kissed her in the magical way he had that had made fireworks rivaling those in the night sky go off inside her chest.

"Liz?"

She opened her eyes and stared into the object of her fantasy's blue eyes. He still looked tired, but it was so wonderful to see him that Liz fought throwing her arms around him. "Adam."

She hadn't seen him since they'd made love. Since he'd held her, kissed her, admitted he needed her. Unfortunately, she barely recognized him as the same man who'd made love to her. He looked grumpy.

"Were you daydreaming?" He frowned, appearing for all the world like he couldn't stand being near her. "Your mind should be on your job."

Liz did a double-take. Not once had Adam or any doctor had cause to complain about her treatment of any of the patients in her care. Not once. Regardless of what was going on, or not going on, between them personally, she hadn't expected him to attack her professionally.

"Pardon?" she asked, thinking that perhaps she'd misread his tone, his look. Maybe she was being overly sensitive because she was so hurt he'd left without waking her.

"Lives are in your hands." He didn't meet her eyes, but instead scribbled something on a notepad. "You shouldn't be daydreaming."

"I wasn't." But she had been, she thought guiltily. Daydreaming about him when he so obviously didn't want her to be.

But why wouldn't he even meet her eyes? Why did she get the impression he was hiding something from her? That he'd been hiding something for weeks? Something beyond his hot and cold attitude toward her?

Yes, he'd left her house without saying her goodbye, but she loved him, wanted him in her life, and wasn't giving up without a fight.

Regardless of what had changed, Adam did have feelings for her. She knew he did. She wasn't going to let whatever was happening between them tear them apart without at least fighting for their relationship.

"Perhaps I was daydreaming just a little," she admitted, giving what she hoped was a bright smile. "Kelly mentioned the Fourth of July and I was thinking back to last year." She willed him to look at her and as if he felt the force of her thoughts, his gaze met hers. "You kissed me for the first time that weekend. Do you remember?"

He looked startled that she hadn't reacted to his antagonistic remark. Had that been what he'd been hoping for? A fight? His mouth opened, but he didn't speak, didn't say whether he remembered or not. No matter, she knew he did. Memories were written all over his face. Memories and emotion. Raw emotion.

His gaze traveled over her face, settled on her lips. He remembered. And wanted to kiss her even now.

She studied his handsome face, the crow's-feet near his eyes that seemed more deeply etched than she recalled, the fatigue weighing down his expression, the bleakness in his eyes that had disappeared when they'd made love. Desperately she wished she could read his mind, know his thoughts, understand what was driving his recent behavior.

"Adam, why didn't you wake me before you left the other morning?"

If she'd shocked him by refusing to fight with him, her blunt question shocked him more. She saw something akin to remorse flicker across his face, but before he answered the unit secretary buzzed her to the room of a patient whose IV machine alarm was sounding. She replaced her beeper and turned to ask Adam if they could grab a bite together and talk when she went on break.

He wasn't there.

Glancing down the hallway, she watched him nod at something Kelly said and disappear with her best friend into a patient's room.

Liz bit into her lower lip. What was going on? Nothing made sense. Adam's actions said one thing, his eyes another.

Her beeper buzzed in her pocket again and with another quick glance toward the room Adam had disappeared into she went to reset Mrs Sanchez's IV.

Kelly at his side, Adam greeted his patient, then paused beside her bed.

How much longer could he do this?

The truth was, he was only delaying the inevitable, but he hadn't been able to utter the words to tell Liz it was over the other night.

He cursed his own weakness, wishing he could blame that, too, on his MS, but he couldn't.

"She's running a low-grade temperature, but all her other vitals are normal." Kelly cut into Adam's self-derision.

How could he have fussed at Liz for daydreaming and then done the same minutes later?

"Dr Cline?" Kelly said again.

He shook off his melancholy and checked his patient, assessing her closely for signs of infection to go along with the temperature. Not finding any, he gave Kelly discharge orders with instructions for the patient to contact his office immediately if her temperature spiked or any new problems developed.

With dread he left the hospital room and prepared to face Liz. Since Kelly, walking beside him and chatting away, said Mrs Arnold was the only one of his patients she had been assigned, the other two must be under Liz's care.

Immediately, he spotted her waiting outside Mrs Arnold's room.

Kelly shot Liz a knowing smile, which Liz nervously returned before meeting Adam's gaze. Kelly elbowed him, then headed toward the nurses' station.

Adam refused to name the emotion pulsing through him at the sight of Liz, standing in the hallway, looking unsure whether to slap him or kiss him.

She was hurt, confused. He could see it on her face, in her golden brown eyes. She deserved so much better than what he was giving her.

"Liz," he started, then paused. He couldn't flat out say they were finished in the middle of the hospital hallway, but he couldn't give her reason to think they'd work through this either.

"Mrs Sanchez is ready to be discharged, but I'm not so sure about Robert Keele," Liz said in a professional tone, her spine straight. However, her gaze couldn't be mistaken for anything other than personal. She wanted to know what was going on and wouldn't sidestep the issues any longer.

He needed to put some distance between them.

"Whether or not Mrs Sanchez is ready to be discharged is for me to decide. Not you."

Liz's eyes widened. She gave him a doe-caught-in-the-headlights stare. A doe who had just been fatally struck by the hunter she'd mistakenly trusted. Him.

He could do this. No matter that his insides wrenched. No matter that his heart felt like it might explode. No matter that he'd rather die than hurt her this way.

She pinned him with her stare. "Have I done something to upset you? I know I've been distracted with Gramps's death. If I've said or done something wrong, I'm sorry."

He cursed the disease running through his body, the disease that made reassuring Liz wrong.

"I've got several patients to see and need to get back to my office for afternoon clinic. We'll talk later." He turned, kept his back as stiff as hers had been, and entered Robert Keele's room.

Determined to focus on his patient rather than the stunned woman he'd left in the hallway, he greeted the man he'd done a hernia repair on earlier that morning. "How's your pain this afternoon?"

"I hurt, but I expected to," the fifty-three-year-old said, scooting up onto his pillow, wincing in the process.

"Be careful," his wife warned from the uncomfortable-looking chair pushed up next to the hospital bed. "You don't want to pop anything open."

"Definitely not," Adam agreed, although he'd done a good job with Robert's procedure and the site wouldn't easily "pop open". He pulled back the thin white blanket so he could check the repair site.

Liz entered the room, but Adam refused to look her way, refused to acknowledge her presence despite every single cell in his body crying out for him to look at her, hold her, love her. He continued to examine Mr Keele and was pleased with what he found.

"I last changed his dressing about thirty minutes ago," Liz said from beside Adam. Her voice was almost emotionless, cluing him in to the fact that she fought tears.

He knew every little nuance about this woman. That she'd learned long ago to keep a tight rein on her emotions when in public, but that tonight her tears would flow. Because of him.

He bit back an apology.

He owed her one. This was his fault. If he had any decency at all he'd tell her it was over and let her get on with her life.

Liz ducked behind the nurses' station and grabbed a stack of papers without looking to see what they were.

"Liz?"

She didn't meet Kelly's eyes.

"Is something wrong?"

She couldn't answer.

"Liz?" Her friend's concern heightened her voice.

"Nothing's wrong. I'm just tired." *And I want to throw up*.

How could the man she'd loved for months act as if she was an inconvenience he wished would go away?

"I don't believe you," Kelly said, her hands on her hips and a determined gleam in her voice. "Tell me what's wrong."

Could a relationship as wonderful as what she and

Adam had shared end just like that? With no warning, no arguments, nothing to make her suspect he had been unhappy? Had she been so caught up in Gramps's illness that she'd missed Adam becoming unhappy with their relationship?

She hiccuped, fighting tears. She couldn't cry. Not at work. She had patients to tend to.

"Liz, look at me right now," Kelly ordered. "You were in Mr Keele's room? Did he remind you of Gramps?"

Liz met Kelly's concerned expression, and proceeded to spring a leak. Two leaks. Leaks that flowed freely down her cheeks, and Kelly hugged her.

"Oh, honey, I'm so sorry. I know how much you miss him."

Another hiccup escaped her mouth. This one carried a half-hysterical edge. Her friend thought she was mourning the loss of her grandfather. In reality she mourned the loss of her best friend and lover, Adam.

"Adam and I are breaking up."

Kelly looked startled. As if Liz's words were the last thing she'd expected to hear. "I know you've been concerned lately, but every couple has arguments. Adam loves you. It'll all work out. You'll see."

But they hadn't argued. She hiccupped again. "He's never said he loves me."

Kelly paused, clearly taken aback by that admission. "Some things don't have to be said with words for them to be true. I've seen how he looks at you. Take it from me, he's crazy about you."

Liz didn't comment, just swiped at unwanted tears.

"He's probably having a bad day and took it out on you," Kelly comforted, giving Liz another quick hug.

"A bad month is more like it." Wiping her palms over her scrub top, Liz pulled herself together. She was stronger than this.

She really had to get her act together. If not internally, she could at least put on a cheery front for her coworkers and patients. They deserved a smiling face and positive attitude. She smiled at her friend, counting her blessings that she had a friend like Kelly in her life. "I'm sorry for blubbering all over you like this."

"No biggie." Kelly gave her a quick hug. "I'm surprised you've held up as well as you have, with your grandfather having been sick so long, and then the long hours you're working, and now Adam. Why are you pulling so many extra hours? When's the last time you had a day off?"

"I've got next Monday and Tuesday off."

"Until HR calls begging you to fill in for whoever isn't coming to work that day." Kelly gave her a knowing look. "Say no for once. Take those days and rest. After you catch up on your sleep things will look brighter."

Liz nodded slowly.

Nausea constricted her throat and, not wanting to alarm Kelly any more than her friend already was, Liz gave her a hug, excused herself, and went to the ladies' room to throw up.

CHAPTER SIX

"HI, MRS PROBST," Adam said, glancing toward the woman sitting on the exam table. He didn't personally know the hospital volunteer, but he'd seen her around the building from time to time.

He'd ask why she was there, but he knew.

Talk of May's tumor could be heard throughout the hospital. He felt partially responsible as she'd originally been scheduled to see him on the day after Gramps had died. When he'd shuffled his schedule to go for the MRI and spinal tap, May had unfortunately been bumped a second time. He hadn't blamed her when he'd heard she'd rescheduled with a different surgeon. Although he wouldn't have chosen the particular one she'd opted to see.

"Dr Cline, this is my husband, John." The woman introduced the man who sat in the chair pushed against the wall. Worry lines furrowed deep above his bushy salt-and-pepper brows.

Adam shook the man's hand.

"You have to know why I'm here," May continued,

her bright eyes meeting Adam's. "I've not kept my problems secret from the hospital staff."

"I was sorry to hear about the tumor, Mrs Probst. And sorry that your appointments with me had to be rescheduled and you were forced to go elsewhere." Adam opened her file, reviewed Dr Mills's surgical notes. Inoperable.

He hated that the evidence pointed toward his having to concur with Dr Mills.

"John and I felt time was of the essence and a week seemed an eternity to wait to find out what was going on inside me."

Adam understood well. Too well. He'd started a three-times-a-week injection yesterday morning that would hopefully slow the progression of his MS, would hopefully stop this exacerbation, prevent new ones from occurring. Waiting to see how he'd respond required patience he wasn't sure he possessed.

"We got a second opinion in Jackson. Actually, a third opinion as well from that surgeon's colleague," her husband interjected. "They won't operate due to May not being strong enough to tolerate surgery." The man's bleak eyes glanced toward his wife. "That's not acceptable to us."

May handed Adam a stack of papers. "These are the office notes from the specialists I saw. Apparently the risk of me dying on the operating table is too high. Both said that at the rate the tumor is growing, I should live another six months, possibly longer."

"Which they say is preferable to her dying now on the operating table," her husband added, giving a pained glance toward his wife.

"Life just to say one is alive is no life at all." May lifted pain-filled eyes to Adam's. "I throw up everything I eat. I've lost thirty pounds in the past two months. I can't sleep, can't do anything because of the way I hurt."

Her husband scooted forward on his seat, took his wife's hand in his and gave a reassuring squeeze. "I love my wife, hate the thought of losing her any sooner than I have to, but she can't go on like this."

"Faced with the option of knowing each day is only going to bring more sickness, that I'm waiting to die, that my family is having to watch me die day after day." Tears filled her eyes, but her head remained high. Her husband lifted her hand to his lips and placed a kiss on her fingers. They exchanged a look of understanding, love, compassion for what the other felt. "Well, like I said," May continued, "that's no life at all."

A cold sweat covered Adam. He knew where this was leading, knew if he put her on the operating table she'd likely die there. No one wanted to operate on the tumor because they may as well write May's obituary. What doctor wanted to be responsible for that?

But if there was a chance to be cured of his MS, wouldn't he take any risk to have that cure? To have that hope for the future?

"Even if there's only a slight chance of me surviving, I'm willing to face those odds. I'd rather die fighting than go on like this, having to see my family watch me suffer, having to suffer this horrible pain." May and her husband both turned expectant eyes toward Adam. "We're here to ask you to please cut this tumor out."

* * *

Liz didn't see or talk to Adam for the next week.

As always, the hospital was understaffed and she'd been able to pull extra shifts. Her next paycheck should make a good dent in Gramps's medical bills.

The nursing director had called early that morning to ask if she'd come in, but when they'd been on the phone the night before, Kelly had threatened her with bodily harm if she didn't take the day off.

Which left her with time on her hands.

First, she cleaned the living room. Then she scrubbed the kitchen until the old ceramic utilities sparkled. Despite brief overly emotional thoughts of stomping the rose bushes to smithereens, she'd trimmed, fertilized, and treated them for insects. All that, and it wasn't even two PM yet.

Perhaps she should eat. She should eat. But almost everything she put in her stomach came back up so she'd fallen into nibbling on toast or crackers.

She wasn't underweight, but the lack of sleep, hours of crying, and another few dropped pounds left her face looking haunted.

She was haunted. Haunted by all the knowing looks her colleagues shot her at work. She'd not breathed a word to anyone except Kelly, but Adam had asked for her not to care for his patients. No one said anything, of course, but they all knew. Word traveled fast.

Unable to keep going over what she'd already spent hours and hours trying to figure out to no avail, Liz headed to the bathroom. She'd give it a good going over as she had the kitchen.

She got the tub, toilet, and sink as spotless as was

humanly possible then decided to clean the small closet. She'd not done much in the way of going through Gramps's things and today was as good as any for getting rid of his toiletries.

She tossed away item after item. When she pulled out a ceramic mug with a shaving brush inside, she sat on the floor and bawled. Memories of, as a child, watching Gramps slather cream onto his strong, cleft chin with the brush and then shave racked her body with grief.

Lord, how she missed him.

Just as she missed the man who'd left her as surely as Gramps had.

Knowing she was preparing for a full-blown pity-party if she sat on the floor a second longer, she reached for a plastic bin of her personal toiletries so she could wipe the shelf down.

When her eyes landed on what the box held she realized what else she'd been missing for…three months.

Liz couldn't believe she was pregnant.

She'd bought two pregnancy kits and both had shown positive. Still, she couldn't believe it. To believe it meant acknowledging that she was pregnant by a man who no longer wanted to be a part of her life.

Personally, she'd decided he'd lost his mind. How else could one explain him going from the perfect lover and companion to his cold-hearted treatment? He hadn't even had the decency to break things off. After a year-long relationship he'd just gone to avoiding her.

Her eyes closed.

Now they were no more and his baby grew inside her.

Adam may not have been willing to love her, but he'd given her something precious. His child.

For the first time in what seemed like for ever, Liz smiled as light-heartedness filled her heart.

"Did you and Adam work things out?" Kelly asked the next morning from behind the nurses' station where they stood talking during a short lull. They'd both taken notes at shift change, been busy with patients, but Liz had caught her friend staring curiously at her several times.

She shook her head, took a sip of the vitamin-packed drink she'd purchased from a vending machine minutes before, and continued with the chart notation she was working on. "I haven't seen Adam since that day here at the hospital."

"You were humming," Kelly accused, leaning against the desk Liz sat at.

That got Liz's attention. Humming? Not lullabies, she hoped since she'd not told a soul of her news. Although she'd used the two home kits and both had showed positive, she wanted her pregnancy confirmed by a gynecologist before she told anyone.

Plus, she'd tell Adam first.

Despite everything, he deserved to hear the news that he was going to be a father before anyone else.

She'd had brief thoughts of packing her things and leaving Robertsville, leaving behind the memories and making a fresh start for herself and the baby without him ever being the wiser that they'd made a baby. But the thoughts had been brief.

Ever the fool, her heart belonged to him and deceiving him so cruelly as to hide their child wasn't something she could do.

And although she should be upset that she was having a baby with a man who'd essentially pushed her out of his life without a word of explanation, she wasn't.

She hadn't thought about having a baby any time soon, had even been on birth control, but she must have missed one at some point when Gramps had been having a bad night. Although she had always thought of motherhood as something far off in her future, the idea of having a baby to love, a child to fill the house with laughter, made her giddy with how blessed she was.

Adam had unknowingly given her what she'd needed. Someone to love and be loved by. Not just someone, their baby.

Would they have a son or a daughter?

She didn't care. Just so long as their baby was healthy.

"Liz? You're doing it again," Kelly interrupted her thoughts.

"Doing what?"

"Smiling. Humming." She arched a brow in question, her gaze narrowed. "It's good to have you back, but what's happened?"

Liz shook her head. "Nothing."

"Don't tell me that. Something's up." Kelly eyed her suspiciously. "Have you met someone new?"

"No." She wanted to tell Kelly her news, but she had to tell Adam first. But she wouldn't be lying to say someone new had entered her life. Someone had. Adam's baby. Kelly had been so worried the past few weeks. She smiled conspiratorially at her friend. "You might say someone's come into my life."

"Oh, Liz!" Kelly exclaimed, looking both shocked and pleased while she hugged her. "This is wonderful news. I'm so relieved. I worried you wouldn't get over Adam. I know how much you cared about him."

She wouldn't get over Adam. Not really. But she would go on and she would have happiness. Knowing about the precious gift inside her removed any doubt that she'd have a bright future.

"I discovered there's room in my heart to love someone besides just Adam Cline, that's all."

Which meant the hell Adam had been through for the past few weeks had all been worth it.

Liz was moving on.

Quicker than he'd expected. Quick enough that a sharp sting burned his chest. Just his pride hurting, he was sure. The fact his vision held a hazy green, well, that was the after-effects of too many hours in the OR, worry over Liz, worry over his MS, worry over what he was going to do about May Probst, and not enough shut-eye. Not jealousy.

Adam swallowed the lump in his throat at the thought of anyone kissing Liz's lips other than him.

"Dr Cline," a patient's wife said from behind him, causing the two oblivious-to-his-presence nurses to jerk toward him. "I'm so glad to see you," the woman continued, unaware of the shock emanating from Liz and Kelly at being overheard. "Herbert's bled through his bandage, and we really weren't expecting that much blood after his hernia repair. I was coming to find his nurse so she could check him, but since you're here, you should."

Herbert, bandage, blood, he mentally noted, but his eyes didn't leave Liz's pink cheeks. She was blushing. *Blushing.*

Her face held guilt.

Blushing cheeks, guilty expression.

Little more than a week ago he'd been in her bed. What had she done since then that would make her react this way?

The sting in his chest intensified, painting his whole world a deep green. A very jealous shade of green.

He should be happy Liz was moving on with her life. Wasn't that what he wanted? For her to find happiness? To find someone who could give her all the things she deserved?

Herbert's wife cleared her throat. "Dr Cline?"

"I'll be by his room in a few minutes to check him, Mrs Donahue. If you'll wait there?"

The woman glanced from Adam to where he stared at the two nurses. Obviously curious, but polite enough not to ask, she nodded. "Thank you, Dr Cline. I'll be in Herb's room."

Willing his eyes away from Liz, Adam pinned Kelly with his glare. "Are you taking care of Herbert Donahue?"

"Angel is," Kelly said, not backing down an inch from her protective stance next to Liz. "But I can check him, if you like. Or do you want me to page Angel?"

He could feel Liz's silky gaze on his features and without meaning to he met her eyes head on.

"Yes." He didn't look away, didn't indicate that he'd answered Kelly's question, just waited.

"Anything else?" Kelly asked, humor in her voice.

Humor that indicated she knew he'd overheard Liz and she knew his secret. He was burning alive inside.

"That'll be all. Thanks." He spun to go to Herbert's room before he made a complete idiot of himself by asking who Liz had been spending her time with.

After all, just because he refused to burden her with a life sentence, that didn't mean just any replacement would do. Liz deserved someone wonderful. Someone who could appreciate her finer qualities. Someone who would rub her aching calves after she'd pulled an extra-long shift. Someone who knew she adored home-made banana pudding from the mom and pop diner they'd occasionally snuck away to. Someone who understood how she'd felt about Gramps.

He was all those things, of course, but he didn't qualify to be Liz's man. Not with his ticking time bomb health.

"I can't believe he didn't even say hello to you," Kelly complained behind his back, having to know he could hear.

"It's OK," Liz replied in a calm voice that hinted she was warning her friend to stay out of it.

"Maybe he needs an antidepressant," Kelly persisted.

"Adam isn't depressed."

He wasn't so sure about that. At the moment, the thought of Liz with another man left him darned depressed.

Moments later, Liz took off toward the nearest exit— which happened to be the front hospital entrance. She could barely catch her breath. Adam had looked upset. Not only that, but she wasn't the only one who'd lost weight. Although the changes were subtle she'd seen the difference in his jaw line, his cheeks, in the way his clothes hung on his body. The question was, why would Adam be losing weight if freedom was what he wanted?

And what was up with the look he'd given her? Could he tell she was hiding something? Had he looked at her and known their baby grew in her belly?

No, she chided herself, Adam didn't know.

He'd been jealous. He hadn't known who he was being jealous of, but he'd definitely been jealous.

Smiling at a visitor coming into the hospital, she exited through the automatic doors. Her heart fluttering, she took off down the sidewalk, not sure where she was headed, just having to get outside the building to process what she'd seen on Adam's face. Even if just for a few minutes during break while Kelly covered her patients.

Adam had looked…possessive. Silly her, seeing him for the first time since learning of their baby, she'd wanted to blurt out the news. Right then and there, she'd wanted to tell him they were having a baby.

She wanted to share with the world how excited she was that she was going to be a mother.

She wanted to be able to share her excitement with Adam. How crazy was that, given the way he'd acted the last time they'd seen each other?

"Liz?"

Liz did a double-take at the frail-looking woman in the wheelchair. If not for the familiar salt-and-pepper-browed man pushing her along the sidewalk she might not have recognized May at all. "May, it's good to see you."

"You, too." Despite her obvious pain and illness, the woman smiled. "You're in a hurry?"

Was she? A minute ago she'd had overwhelming claustrophobia, but seeing May so deteriorated in such a short time, Liz didn't have the heart to rush on. "Not really. I stepped out for fresh air while taking my break."

May glanced around at the well-tended hospital lawn and Liz followed her gaze, taking in their surroundings. Multicolored Binkas bloomed all along the mulched flower-beds. A few butterflies danced from bloom to bloom, seemingly without a care in the world.

How easy it was in life to forget to stop to enjoy the beauty of the moment, to smell the roses, so to speak. Not that Liz could smell the flowers over the stifling aroma of the nearby fast-food restaurants that were nestled into the lot next to the hospital.

"We passed by your house on our way to a prayer meeting last evening. Your grandfather's rosebushes are as lovely as ever."

Had May read her mind?

"Gramps loved those roses," Liz said wistfully, recalling many a day when her grandfather had tended the demanding flowers. When he'd still been able to. Then he'd tediously instructed her on their care.

"I always was jealous of those gorgeous blooms. Never could get mine to look the way his did. Few can." Her gaze softened. "You're very much like him, you know."

"Thank you." Liz beamed. She couldn't have been paid a nicer compliment.

Catching her breath in a sharp gasp, May's face pinched in pain. Her hands gripped her wheelchair for a few moments before she returned her gaze to Liz.

"We should be going," May's husband reminded her

from where he stood behind the wheelchair. "Your appointment is in fifteen minutes."

Liz wanted to ask more, to discover who May was seeing, but her expression was so hollow that she didn't want to delay her. She'd seen Dr Mills's notes. He'd recommended May to see a pain specialist to ease her suffering and improve the quality of her remaining days. Perhaps that's where she was headed.

Knowing what it was like to watch someone suffer as they waited to die, Liz's heart went out to May and John.

She stooped, kissed May's cheek. "Thank you for your kind words about Gramps. I always feel closer to him when I speak with you. Take care of yourself, and if there's anything I can do, anything at all, let me know."

The couple nodded, then John pushed his wife toward the hospital entrance.

Liz made a mental note to prepare a meal for the Probsts. She'd stop by, visit, offer to help with cleaning or shopping. Even the most mundane things could seem difficult when one was seriously ill.

Yes, she'd definitely stop by to visit with the Probsts and perhaps by then she'd be able to share her wonderful news with the couple.

CHAPTER SEVEN

SEVEN hours in the operating room and still going, Adam paused long enough for the nurse to swab his forehead. He was sweating like hell. Tired as hell. Numb as hell.

His fingertips had little feeling left in them, to the point he battled whether or not he should close May up and call it quits.

No, if he and the two other surgeons—one vascular and one nephrologist—didn't finish the job, May had no hope.

Not to mention the hospital board would possibly suspend him since they'd barely given their approval for him to go ahead.

Never in his career at Robertsville had he had to ask permission to operate on a patient. The board had called him to task the moment he'd scheduled May's surgery. Called a meeting that had been more about Dr Mills's arrogance than real concern for the patient. Called a meeting that had delayed May's surgery longer than Adam liked. With each day that had passed, she'd weakened.

So far she was holding her own. Only once had her

blood pressure dropped. They'd administered a vaso-
constrictor, increased her fluids, and she'd steadied out.
They'd also given her several bags of packed red blood
cells because of the amount of blood she'd lost. But she
was doing better than anyone could have predicted. That
could change in a heartbeat.

In the slip of a numb finger.

"You OK?" the nurse assisting him asked, causing
the vascular surgeon to glance toward Adam.

He could do this. For May. If he stopped…

"Fine." Adam nodded and continued the tedious task
of removing the entangled tumor from May while the
other surgical teams worked simultaneously. He used
sight to guide his way when the sensation in his fingers
failed him. Thank God his vision wasn't as blurred as
it was at times.

An hour later, Adam surveyed his work. Not all of
the tumor was gone, but the bulk of the mass had been
removed, along with numerous branches. Unfortunately
May's right kidney and ureter had also been cut out as
they hadn't been able to save them. The tumor had been
too embedded into the tissue.

Amazingly, the surgery was a success. The only thing
left was finishing touches.

Touches he wasn't able to do.

He couldn't feel his left hand, his head hurt like hell,
and he'd started squinting to sharpen his vision. To go
further was a risk he couldn't take.

He turned to the vascular surgeon. "You OK to finish
up without me?"

Surprised, Dr Robards nodded and continued what
he was doing. Adam stepped away.

His head spun and he swayed.

"Dr Cline?" the nurse said from right beside him. "Dr Cline, are you OK?"

No, Adam wasn't.

He couldn't see a damned thing out of his right eye. From that eye, the world had gone black.

Having arranged for another physician to cover the ER for a few hours until he returned, Adam's friend Larry drove him to the hospital in Jackson. Fortunately he didn't ask too many questions. Without Adam having to say a thing, Larry knew.

Of course, it had been his friend who'd first diagnosed his MS. His friend who'd called the neurologist Adam had been seeing and begged him to see Adam that evening as a special favor.

Larry who'd asked if he should call Liz.

If anything, what had happened today proved that he'd done the right thing to push Liz away. What if his sight hadn't returned? What if both eyes had gone blind and stayed that way? Sure, he would eventually have learned to cope, but Liz would have been stuck with the fallout. Stuck with a man who wasn't the man she deserved.

He loved her too much to saddle her with that.

"The temporary blindness was from extreme fatigue, Adam. You've been pushing yourself too hard. I know Dr Winters told you there was no reason you couldn't continue to work, but taking on a case on like May Probst's was insane."

"I have cut back on my hours," Adam reminded. He'd cut his former workload by a third. His staff and colleagues all thought it had to do with his and Liz's problems. Just as they must think his haggard appearance was related to his personal problems.

Oh, yeah, he'd cut back. Not that he'd had much rest. Instead, he'd dream of Liz, of the days when he'd been healthy, and he'd thought he'd grow old at her side.

"But you still pulled something stupid," Larry continued. "You know better."

Doing May's surgery was stupid according to the hospital board, but letting a woman die without attempting desired treatment, well, that was downright cruel in Adam's eyes. Particularly at the moment.

What he wouldn't give for even a slim chance of something healing him, what he'd be willing to risk for that chance—everything.

"And now everyone knows something is wrong with me." Adam sighed. He'd almost passed out in the OR. Had literally sat down on the OR floor. Which really had been stupid as he'd distracted everyone from May. Thank God she'd done well.

Perhaps part of him had been rebellious, fighting against diseases that robbed life. By taking on May's case he'd somehow felt empowered, as if he had been striking out at his own body's ailments.

"They'll probably write it off as fatigue, stress over May's surgery, or on your problems with Liz. Perhaps even blame it on a hypoglycemic reaction since you'd been in surgery so long."

"Perhaps," Adam agreed. He hated anyone thinking him incapable. Hated the thought that he'd been numb and blind for what had seemed like for ever but in actuality had only been a couple of minutes.

"If Dr Winters doesn't put you on medical leave, I want you to take a few days off work, Adam. Get some rest."

Rest. What a joke. "I'll go crazy if I have to sit at home doing nothing."

"Then take a vacation. Go play golf. Go on a cruise. Make up with Liz. Please, make up with Liz. Let her help you through this."

He ignored the making-up-with-Liz suggestion. Ignored the pang that went along with the thought she might be with someone else this very minute, laughing, smiling, sharing dinner, more.

"Fine, I'll rest." Today had scared him more than he liked to admit, but not nearly as much as the thought of how he'd react the first time he saw Liz with another man. How would he contain what he had no right to feel? "But not until after I finish this week's schedule. I've already rescheduled appointments too many times over the past month."

His friend shot him a glance from the driver's side of the car. "Dr Winters may put you on medical leave, Adam. I hope he does. If he asks my opinion, that's what I'm going to tell him."

"Which is why you won't be invited into the exam room when he examines me."

Larry glared.

"Actually," Adam conceded, "my schedule is fairly light. I'd given myself time…in case things didn't go well with my injections."

Larry shook his head. "And they say nurses make bad patients. Surgeons are far worse."

* * *

Late that night Liz paced across her living room and racked her brain for clues as to what she should say to Adam.

She'd exchanged work days with another nurse today and gone for her doctor's appointment that morning. Not only had Dr Saunders confirmed her pregnancy, she'd listened to the baby's heartbeat with an ultrasonic Doppler that had allowed her to listen as well.

Their child had a strong, steady heartbeat.

Almost giddy with the confirmation, with the affirmation given by listening to that heartbeat, she'd made a casserole and some goodies and stopped by the Probsts' home. Once there she'd learned from a neighbor that May wasn't home, had been in surgery that day.

She'd called the hospital to check on her, but had only been told that May was holding her own.

Adam had operated.

The board had only given its OK grudgingly.

He'd put his career on the line to attempt to save a woman's life.

Because it was the right thing to do.

That was the Adam she loved.

The Adam who'd stood by her side many a long night caring for her grandfather, who'd stood by her side at his funeral, who'd fathered her baby.

Adam's baby.

The weather had turned drizzly, but she was too wound up to sit at home.

Not when she wanted to scream her news to the world. She was having Adam's baby!

Now that she had the lab slip from Dr Saunders there

wasn't any reason to prolong telling him. OK, so the weather was a little foggy, but not too bad.

Her silly heart was racing again. Probably because of worry about Adam's reaction.

She loved Adam, never wanted to see him hurt, and when she thought back on the last time she'd seen him, he had looked hurt.

He'd looked jealous, but hurt had also shone in his eyes. Tormented hurt almost.

Why would Adam be hurt? She'd reached out repeatedly only to have him push her away time and again.

For the life of her she couldn't figure out what might have changed. Then again, those first few days following Gramps's death she'd moved in a fog. Perhaps she'd said something out of line. Something that had hurt Adam and made him step away from the closeness they'd shared.

What of his distraction? The times she'd caught him rubbing his temple? Had that only been a stress reaction? A headache?

She only knew one way to find out. The same way Adam was going to find out about the wonderful blessing they'd been given. She had to tell him.

She glanced at her watch. It was late, after ten. Adam would be home, unless he'd been called into the emergency room or one of his patients had a problem. If he had been called to the hospital, she'd wait for him to return.

Slipping on a pair of sandals, Liz grabbed her purse and car keys.

The heavy fog oppressing the night made the drive even more harried, caused the muscles between her shoulders to tighten.

Twenty tense minutes later she stood outside Adam's front door, her confidence wavering. What if he refused to let her in? What if he turned her away? What if he said he didn't care that she was pregnant with his baby?

She placed her palm protectively over her abdomen. She wanted this baby so much. How could he not want a baby he'd help create?

She knocked on the door and waited. And waited some more.

She knocked again. Louder this time.

She heard movement inside the condo, heard footsteps.

When the door opened, she sighed in relief, knowing she'd been right to come.

Adam looked terrible, as if he'd lost his whole world.

Was he dreaming that Liz was standing on his doorstep?

No, there was too much uncertainty in her eyes for this to be a dream. In his dreams he'd be free to take her in his arms and never let her go. His vision wouldn't be blurred—although blurred was a hell of a lot more preferable to total blackout—and his fingertips wouldn't feel like they were on fire. His legs wouldn't hurt, wouldn't feel as if they might go out from under him.

"You shouldn't be here." His voice came out gruffer than he'd meant it to. Mostly because he was so tired, so frustrated with the lot he'd been dealt.

He wasn't sure he was strong enough tonight to face Liz and not take her in his arms. Hadn't he already done that on the day he'd had his MS confirmed?

He'd gone, full of liquid courage, and shown up on her doorstep to gallantly tell her it was over. Only he'd wanted to cry in her arms like a little boy, wanted to lose his sorrows in the safety of her arms.

She'd welcomed him, loved him, helped him face that night.

Now she was here, on his doorstep, on a night when he faced demons. Demons of fatigue. Demons of having been blind. Demons of the fear that clawed at his psyche about what the future held for him.

"Go home, Liz."

Her eyes widening, she took a step back and lost her balance. Automatically he grasped her arm to keep her from falling. Heat sizzled through him at the contact. A heat much hotter than the flame his disease burned his soul with. When she steadied, her gaze dropped to where he held her arm. Did her pulse throb at that contact the way his did?

She took a deep breath, searched his face for reassurance he couldn't give. "We need to talk, Adam. You know we do."

She was right. He'd delayed this conversation too long already.

"You're right."

"Don't sound so excited to see me," she murmured as she walked past him, entering his condo.

How could he explain how weak he felt?

"Forgive me, but I'm too tired to stand," she said, sitting on his sofa.

Despite the energy with which she'd stormed into his house, Liz did look tired. Her hair was pulled up in a ponytail, drawing attention to her puffy eyes. She looked exhausted.

As exhausted as he felt and probably looked, too.

His heart squeezed. "You should be home in bed. Not knocking on my door in the middle of the night."

"I've been patient, Adam, for weeks. Now's the time to clear the air between us." She glanced around his living room, letting her gaze settle momentarily to a snapshot of them that rested on his mantel. Why hadn't he gotten rid of that photo? Why had he been sitting on the sofa blankly staring at it before Liz's knocking had broken into his reverie?

"We have things that need to be said." Her gaze didn't leave the happy couple in the print. They'd been at a hospital picnic celebrating twenty years of business in the community. Kelly had taken the photo and given him and Liz framed prints.

He loved this woman and it showed in that picture. Just as her feelings for him showed. Life had been near wonderful with the exception of Gramps. How had things gotten so out of control?

Shaking inside, Adam sat on the opposite end of the sofa. He didn't want to hurt Liz.

"We should let things end without getting messy."

She paled at his "let things end", but kept her chin high. "Things are already messy, Adam. More so than you realize."

He wasn't strong enough, not tonight. He needed her to leave, needed her not to make doing the right thing more difficult. "Why are you doing this?"

"Because I care," she said point blank, not budging an inch.

"You shouldn't."

"Why wouldn't I care about you? You were my boy-friend, my best friend, my lover." Her whiskey-colored eyes penetrated him. "Actually, I thought we were more than that."

"I thought you'd met someone else."

Her gaze searched his and she started to say one thing, visibly changed her mind, then said, "I love you, Adam. I have for months and imagine I still will until I draw my last breath."

"Liz." How could he convince her she was better off without him?

"You must have realized how I feel about you. Other than Gramps, you're the only man I've ever loved."

Why was she telling him this? He didn't need to hear this, didn't need to know what might have been.

"I'm sorry, Liz. What we had was fun, but I'm not in love with you, nor do I want to be."

Her gaze lowered to her lap and her throat worked, as if she had a difficult time making his words go down. "You don't love me? You're sure?"

Liz deserved a wonderful life, to fall in love with someone who would cherish her, take care of her, give her the whole world. He couldn't deprive her of that.

"No, Liz." He met her eyes, forced himself to hold steady, to remember he was doing this for her. "I don't. I never have, and I never will."

She glared at him, suspicion in her eyes. "If you don't love me and never have, tell me what's changed? Why your attitude went from caring and wonderful to ignoring me almost overnight? If you didn't love me all along, what was the difference? Why couldn't we just keep going on as we were?"

It was a logical question and one he struggled to answer.

"After Gramps's funeral seemed like the right time to make a break."

Liz closed her eyes, inhaled a deep breath, visibly trembled. Better to hurt for a day or two now than to get stuck with him every day and night for the rest of her life.

"I'm sorry, Liz." He was sorry he'd put her in this position. For that alone she should hate him.

"The past year has been an aberration, but it wasn't real. Not for me. Your grandfather's funeral made me realize you're a free woman now, ready to move on with the rest of your life." Lord, he sounded sincere. Like he believed what he said. She sat in silence staring at her hands, hands that trembled in her lap. "It wouldn't be right for me to hold you back when I have no desire for our relationship to go further."

"Hold me back?"

"You should move on with your life, date other men."

A soft hiccup escaped from her lips and she attempted to hide the tell-tale motion by covering her mouth with her hand.

"Because you want to date other women?" Her voice sounded frail, lost.

No, he wanted to scream, he only wanted her. But prolonging the inevitable only made this all the harder. They needed a clean break. Liz needed to be free.

"Yes."

Another hiccup.

More guilt hit him, but he pressed onward, knowing he had to end this tonight. "If I gave you reason to believe I cared more for you, it was unintentional."

"Unintentional?" Her lost expression turned angry. "Making love to me was unintentional? What about the other night, Adam? Did our love-making mean nothing to you?"

The night in question blazed through his mind like a fiery brand. He'd forever imprinted his memory with her that night. Everything about her from her taste to her softness to her sweet responses to his body. Everything.

"That was just sex, Liz," he lied.

"Just sex?" She scoffed. "You're insane. That wasn't just sex."

"How would you know?" He hit her where he knew it would hurt. "I'm the only man you've been with. I'd say I'm a better judge of what's between us physically, and it's just sex."

Unlike any sex he'd ever had, but somehow telling Liz she was phenomenal and made him feel like he could leap tall buildings and save the world didn't seem appropriate, given current circumstances.

"You're saying because I haven't slept around I don't know what I feel?"

"I understand you're upset, but arguing about this isn't going to change anything."

She curled her fingers into fists. "Tell me the truth, Adam, what's going on with you? Because I don't buy this. None of this fits."

"I'm sorry you can't accept that we're over, Liz."

Her entire body trembled, but she held herself together. Just like she always did. Gramps's death and funeral had been the only times he'd ever seen her so shaken. Liz would be OK, would get over him, and find the life she deserved.

"OK," she agreed, lifting her shoulders in a brave gesture.

OK, she would be OK, get over him, and find the life she deserved.

"But you'll have to explain how this works."

"How what works?" She'd totally lost him.

"Us."

"There is no us. Not any more."

"So we pretend we don't know each other? You're going to keep ignoring me? Act like we never meant anything to each other?" Pink crept into her cheeks. "I mean, that you meant something to me," she amended, with a slight sarcastic edge to her voice.

"We can still be friends."

She picked up a burgundy-colored square cushion from the corner of the sofa and threw it at him. Hard.

He didn't attempt to block the pillow from hitting him in the chest. He expected a tongue-lashing to accompany the blow.

But she didn't. Instead, she stood, wiped her hands over her faded jeans, and took a deep breath. "If this is what you want, fine. But don't ask me to be your friend, Adam. Hopefully I can be someday, but not now, because right now I think I hate you for dragging this out. For not telling me weeks ago that you didn't want me in your life when you knew we were over. How dare you let me think you cared for me?"

He nodded his understanding, wondering why he didn't feel better that his plan was working. Liz was starting to move away from him. He should pat himself on the back for a job well done. Instead, he felt like giving in to the gaping hole in his chest.

She turned away, but not before he saw the tears streaming down her cheeks.

He caught up with her as she reached the front door, placed his hand on her shoulders just as she grasped the knob. "Don't go like this."

"Like what?" she asked in mid-hiccup, not looking at him.

"Upset. Be reasonable. You don't need to drive until you calm down."

"Reasonable?" She spun and faced him. Her eyes narrowed to livid golden flames. "Don't you tell me about reasonable, because I'll tell you what I think is reasonable. Reasonable is spending a year of your life loving a man and having a wonderful, albeit limited relationship with that man. When life lifts those limits, thinking you have a future with that man, thinking you will someday marry, raise a family together. That's reasonable. You playing games with my heart, that's what's not reasonable."

His insides shook from the enormity of the emotions rushing through him. He could never have a family with Liz, never have a family period. What if he passed on this horrible disease to an innocent child?

"I never led you to believe we had a future together," he reminded her. She loved him and that was yet another reason he had to let her go.

"Didn't you?"

Her two words echoed around the room, around his heart.

"Liz," he sighed, not able to stand her pain. "Don't do this to us."

"Have you forgotten? There is no us." With that she raced out the door and into the foggy night.

* * *

Liz had never been much of a crier, but she'd cried until she hadn't thought she'd had any tears left on the day Gramps had died and on the day that followed, but she'd been wrong. She'd had lots of tears left. Seas full. Adam had proved that to her time and again these past weeks. She could only assume hormones caused her weepiness.

Either that or her broken heart.

She wiped at her eyes, cursing both her tear-blurred vision and the thick fog obscuring the road. She was sure the fog hadn't been this heavy when she'd driven to Adam's. Otherwise she'd never have come to his place tonight.

No, that wasn't true. She'd been in a bad way, needing to tell him about their baby. She would have confronted him tonight regardless. She'd dealt with a mother who'd run out on her years ago and a father who'd never cared enough to be a part of her life.

Adam had rejected her, too. He didn't love her. He'd said he didn't, told her to her face. Why did his words feel so wrong? Surely she hadn't thought he had to love her just because she loved him? Just because he'd made love to her so sweetly, so tenderly?

All those times he'd held her, kissed her, made her feel alive when she'd felt dead inside, it had all been in the name of sex.

One didn't spend a year with someone because of sex. Did they? If not for sex, then why? Why had he been hers exclusively for so long if he wasn't into commitment?

She blinked, clearing her eyes and wishing her windshield wipers could clear the fog shrouding her view.

God, she just wanted to get home, curl up in bed in the room she'd slept in since the age of four. The room she'd made love to Adam in just last week when she'd hoped things would go back to being wonderful between them.

She'd recognized the wild desperation in him.

He'd known that night would be their last.

What didn't make sense was why he'd be so desperate when he was the one bringing the relationship to an end.

Tears blurred her eyes again. Even had they not, Liz wasn't sure she could have missed the deer that leapt in front of her car and sent her careening off the highway.

CHAPTER EIGHT

IN SLOW increments Liz became aware of her surroundings. Bright lights shone above her face, making opening her eyes difficult. Or maybe it was the pounding in her head that made the slightest movement seem impossible.

Although the light gave off heat, her insides felt cold. Too cold. Almost as if she were buried in snow.

The thought filled her with panic, panic she would have thought vivid enough to push her into motion, but nothing happened. No flailing arms. No kicking. No screaming. No anything.

Summoning all her strength, she forced one eye open, then the other, and flinched from the intensity of the light shining over her.

"Liz?" her friend Mona, an ER nurse, asked. "Can you hear me, Liz?"

Of course she could hear her. She would have told her but speaking required more energy than she could find. Odd, that.

"Liz?"

Liz looked beyond Mona's worried face to where she

focused on Dr Larry Graviss's face. The emergency room doctor's eyes narrowed.

"Liz?" Why was he looking so intently at her? "If you can hear me, blink your eyes."

Blink her eyes?

Why Adam's friend would ask her to do that she couldn't comprehend, but she'd play along with whatever game her coworkers had going. She tried to blink, but her eyes didn't co-operate.

"Liz," Mona said softly. "Blink your eyes, honey."

Honey? What was with that? Her friend since nursing school never called her honey. But Mona waited patiently for an eye blink. Focusing all her energy on her eyes, Liz blinked.

"Oh, Liz." With an emotional gasp, Mona covered her mouth with her hand. She looked ready to cry. "Thank goodness. You can hear us."

Did they think she couldn't? Liz wanted to look away as Dr Graviss shone a light in her eyes…almost as if he was checking her pupil reflexes.

The deep cold inside her body began to thaw, leaving her brain fuzzy. Although she was sure she meant to confront her coworkers to find out what was going on, she closed her eyes and drifted into sweet nothingness.

A nothingness where Gramps was still alive, healthy. A nothingness where Adam loved her with all his heart, and they'd be a happy family.

Adam tore into the emergency room without bothering to stop to ask where Liz was. There were only six bays in the Robertsville emergency department. He'd find her quicker than someone could tell him.

The moment he entered the emergency room, he caught sight of Mona Davenport. Mona and Liz had gone through nursing school together and the petite brunette was one of Liz's friends. He could tell she'd been crying. The lost look on her face twisted his insides.

"Where is she?"

Mona glanced toward bay two. "You can't go back there."

"Why the hell not?"

Mona winced. "Dr Graviss wants to talk with you."

All the horrible scenarios he'd envisioned during the hellish drive to the hospital washed over him anew.

"She's dead, isn't she?" Why else would Larry want to talk to him first? His knees wobbled beneath him, threatening to give way and dump him on the hospital floor. He'd lost Liz. For ever.

Mona's eyes closed, her mouth compressing while she appeared to be trying to pull herself together.

His heart turned inside out. Fate couldn't be that cruel, couldn't snatch Liz away. Couldn't have his last moments shared with her be of him hurting her, telling her he didn't love her when she'd poured out her heart.

Liz couldn't be gone when she had so much life to live. When the only reason he'd pushed her away was so she could live that life. Not die thinking he hadn't cared.

He cared. God, how he cared. Enough that he'd let her go so she could have a life.

"She's not dead, Adam," the nurse said slowly, failing to hide her own pain. "She's banged up really bad, going in and out of consciousness, but she's alive."

What Mona was saying registered. Liz was alive.

He made a beeline for bay two. He had to see for

himself. Had to tell her…what? That he was a selfish fool and wanted her in his life always? That he couldn't bear the thought of a world without her in it? That he'd thought he had to follow that old adage of "If you love someone you'll set them free"?

Adam pushed the curtain back, but the hospital bed was empty. Mona stepped up behind him. "I told you that Dr Graviss wants to talk to you first," she reminded him.

"Where is she?" He spun, facing the sniffling nurse who was dabbing her eyes with a tissue.

Mona sighed, gave him an empathetic look. "She's having tests done to assess her head injuries."

"She hit her head?"

The police officer who'd come to his house hadn't been able—or willing—to share the details of Liz's crash. Since she was going in and out of consciousness a head injury made sense.

"Against the steering-wheel," Mona said. "I can't figure out exactly what happened. Liz wouldn't have been driving without her seatbelt on a night like tonight."

He'd done this to her.

In trying to protect her, he'd hurt her emotionally and physically.

Adam walked over to the computer, punched in his access code and pulled up Liz's chart to discover the extent of her injuries.

"Adam, you know you're not supposed to look at Liz's record. Close her chart for both our sakes," Mona said from directly behind him.

"I want to know what's going on. If Liz is in Radiology, I'm assuming she's somewhat stable."

"Her vitals were holding with no evidence of internal

bleeding, if that's what you're asking." Mona shook her head. "I really shouldn't be telling you any of this. You're not family, neither do you have a signed release that grants you knowledge about Liz."

He gave the nurse a scalding look.

"You need to close her file. Now." Mona stood her ground. "It's against hospital policy for you to look at Liz's chart." Mona sighed, her momentary bravado wilting before his eyes. "I understand how you feel," she said. "I felt so helpless when she just kept lying there unresponsive after the paramedics brought her in."

He winced at the vision her words elicited. The vision that matched his thoughts of losing Liz for ever.

When the knock on the door had come, he'd thought Liz had come back and he'd been filled with mixed emotions. Elation and dread. Elation that she cared enough to fight for him, that she wanted a future with him that much. Dread that he'd have to hurt her again because he had no future.

When the officer had identified himself, he'd been filled with total dread. Police officers didn't make house calls during the night unless something bad had happened.

The officer explained there'd been an accident. Liz had lost control of her car and smashed into a tree. She'd been taken to Robertsville Hospital by ambulance and they were contacting him because he was listed as her emergency contact in her wallet. The policeman hadn't been able to tell him more. Not even whether or not Liz was alive.

The hurt in Liz's eyes when she'd last looked at him had haunted his entire drive to the hospital.

Mona was still talking, he realized. He'd caught the word "condition" a couple of times but not much more.

"Adam, close Liz's chart, or I'm going to report you to the hospital administrator," she threatened.

He glared. Not that he was afraid of being reported. He wasn't. But he couldn't blame Mona for doing her job. She was right. He had no right to access Liz's chart.

"I can't just stand here waiting for Liz to return to the emergency room," he said out loud, having an entirely different perspective of how family members felt as they waited for news of their loved ones.

"Kelly's here. I called her right after they brought Liz in. She's gone for coffee. Maybe you could join her," Mona suggested softly, placing her hand on his upper arm and giving a reassuring squeeze. "I'll page you the moment Liz returns."

Liz was pretty sure someone had mistaken her for an American football player. Because she'd been tackled by a three-hundred-pound lineman. Repeatedly.

Her head hurt, her chest hurt, and her leg hurt.

"Stay with me, Liz," Dr Graviss ordered from somewhere to her right. His words didn't make sense, which was strange as he was usually direct and to the point. She'd always admired that about the emergency medicine physician who was one of Adam's closest friends.

She opened her eyes again, squinted at his fuzzy blond hair, and vaguely wondered what had happened to the bright light. "Where am I?"

"In Radiology. You regained consciousness while a CT scan was being performed on you."

"A CT scan?" She tried to sit up and realized she

couldn't. That she couldn't even move her arms. "Something's wrong with my body."

Dr Graviss took her hand and squeezed. "You're strapped down to the table to cut down on motion noise on your scan." He released a Velcro strap, but Liz still couldn't lift her arms. They were too heavy.

"How much do you remember, Liz?" he asked gently.

"About what?"

"Tonight."

"What happened tonight?"

"That's what I'm hoping you can tell me."

Liz tried to think, tried to remember why she'd be in Radiology with Dr Graviss. Neither of them belonged in the radiology department.

"Where is she?" A familiar voice broke into her thoughts. Adam.

Warmth filled her. Her gaze went in the direction from which she'd heard his voice.

He barged into the room with Mona in his wake tugging on his shirt, fussing at him. Why was her friend fussing at Adam? Mona knew Adam was wonderful, was her rock to keep her steady. That he was the father of her baby.

No, Mona didn't know that. No one did.

That's when everything hit her.

Adam's avoidance, Adam's treatment of her, using her for one-last-time sex, telling her he didn't love her and wanted to date other women.

Her gaze met his and she saw concern that for a moment made her think his words had been lies. That she'd been right all along, and he did love her. Fool. She berated her naivety. When was she going to learn?

Adam didn't love her. Why would he lie about the way he felt? She'd told him she loved him so it couldn't be fear of not knowing how she felt. No, she didn't see love. What she saw reflected in his concerned eyes wasn't real.

Very simply, he felt guilt.

Guilt because she'd been in a car accident.

A car accident.

Her baby. She wanted to touch her stomach but couldn't. Had the crash hurt the precious life inside her?

"Oh, God, tell me I'm OK," she demanded in a panicked voice.

"You're OK, Liz," Dr Graviss assured from her side, ignoring Adam's intrusion. "You were in a car accident."

"A deer ran in front of me." Those few seconds before losing consciousness replayed in her mind. She'd been so afraid, thinking she was going to die, that she'd never hold her baby. She fought hyperventilating by taking controlled breaths. "I swerved to miss the deer and lost control of my car. Did I…" She paused, glanced toward Adam and hesitated before asking, "Hit the deer?"

Adam ignored Mona's continued protests at his intrusion into the radiology department. He'd had to see Liz for himself.

His gaze ate her up, assessing each section of her body. She wore a thin cotton hospital gown that tied together at the back. Scrapes and bruises littered her arms and legs, but her face boasted the largest visible lesion. One that covered a large section of her right forehead. A gash that had been closed with a row of neat stitches.

He moved closer, straining to hear what she said, and

the scent of blood made his head swim. The scent of Liz's blood.

Her life could have been snuffed out just like that.

"I'm not sure, Liz." Larry leaned close, looking Liz directly in the eyes while he spoke to her. "No one mentioned a deer. You were brought to the hospital by ambulance. Do you remember?"

Liz's eyes closed. Her face pinched with pain, pinched with trying to recall the events that had occurred that night. "I remember crashing into the tree."

What else did she remember? Did she recall that he'd been the biggest fool ever to walk the face of the earth? That all this was his fault?

"But nothing after that," she continued. "Tell me I'm OK. Please."

"Tell her she's OK," Adam demanded, needing to hear the confirmation himself. Liz would be OK. She had to be.

Larry glanced up from Liz, met his gaze, and frowned. "Adam," he acknowledged. "You're not on duty and should have waited out front. Not to mention that you should be home in bed. *Resting.*"

"The hell you say." He wasn't going anywhere. Not until he was sure Liz was going to be OK.

He could have lost her for ever.

Just like that, and all his worrying about the future, about burdening Liz, would have been for naught.

"Oh, Liz." He took her hand in his and gave a gentle squeeze, but she didn't respond to his action, didn't even look at him.

Instead, she kept beseeching eyes on Larry. "Make him leave."

Stunned by her soft plea, Adam let go of Liz's hand.

Her limp arm fell to the table she lay on. She wanted him to leave?

"Please," she said. Her heart monitor beeped rapidly as her pulse rate increased. "Make him go. I can't deal with him right now. I just want him gone."

She didn't want him here? Just hours ago she had been in his condo, telling him she loved him. Now she didn't want him in the same room?

Larry gave him a sympathetic look. "It would be better if you waited outside, Adam. I need to finish examining Liz so the radiology tech can finish her tests."

He was being asked to leave. By Liz. By Larry.

She didn't understand and he had to make her. Had to tell her that he loved her, always had, and that everything he'd done had been because he'd believed it was the right thing for her.

"Liz," he began, but she refused to look at him, just kept her gaze trained on Larry's face.

"Please," she said a third time, tears in her eyes. "I don't want him here."

"You're upsetting her, Adam," Larry needlessly informed Adam. "Wait outside."

Adam wanted to argue, but logically Liz needed medical care. His interference was only slowing down her examination and tests. Unfortunately logic was in short supply when Liz was lying injured on the table.

But he stepped out. After dropping a kiss on Liz's good cheek and whispering something to her, Mona followed.

"You shouldn't have barged in there," she scolded, but gave him a reassuring pat on his arm.

"I had to see her."

"And now that you've seen? Now what?" Kelly demanded from a few feet away, gripping a cup of coffee tightly in her hand, like she really wanted to throw it at him. "You had no right to interrupt Liz's care, not after the past few weeks. You've hurt her so much."

Apparently, Kelly had been waiting outside the room for Liz's tests to finish and resented it that he'd interrupted. He shouldn't have, but he'd had to see her. Not that he was sure he could make her, make anyone, understand the conflicting emotions running through him.

Mona watched them curiously.

He raked his fingers through his hair. "I'd never intentionally hurt Liz."

But that wasn't true. He had intentionally hurt her because he was saving her from a greater pain at a later time. Or so he'd thought.

The memory of how fragile she'd appeared on the radiology table flashed through his mind, and he winced. Damn it. He never wanted Liz to hurt.

"Yet you'd do this to her? Knowing…" Her hand covered her mouth but her eyes shone with grave disappointment. "I'd thought better of you."

Kelly gave him a dirty look, downed her coffee, crumpled the cup the way she probably wanted to crumple him. She walked away, but not without tossing a dirty name over her shoulder.

He didn't contest her assessment of his character.

He had hurt the woman he loved. Hurt her deeply.

He deserved every negative thing her friend said.

Several hours later Adam rolled his throbbing forehead against the cold concrete of the hospital wall. What was taking Kelly and Mona so long? They'd been in the ICU room Liz had been admitted to for over an hour. Wasn't Mona on duty in the emergency room?

All he wanted was a few minutes with Liz, but her self-appointed watchdogs didn't want him "upsetting her". Although he'd gotten a look while she'd been in Radiology, until he checked her himself from head to toe he wasn't going to be satisfied.

If she would agree to see him.

What if she didn't? What if she refused to give him the chance to say how sorry he was?

To tell her that when the officer had shown up on his doorstep, all he'd been able to think of had been getting to Liz? Of telling her how much he loved her and needed her in his life?

"What are you still doing here? Didn't I tell you to go home and rest?"

Adam straightened, turned to meet Larry's eyes. He hadn't heard the doctor come up the hallway, had been too lost in his own thoughts. "Would you leave without seeing Liz if you were me?"

"Probably not, but she doesn't need to be upset," Larry repeated Mona and Kelly's warnings.

Did everyone think he planned to go in and cause a fight? Surely they knew him better than that?

"She's been through a great deal and has lost consciousness again. She has a concussion and her ankle is broken. Whatever's going on between the two of you, and I have a horrible suspicion I know exactly what it is, tonight isn't the time to go into it."

"You should mind your own business," Adam started,

then rubbed his jaw at Larry's pointed look. "The truth is," he admitted, "I told her we were finished."

Larry's brows rose and he gave a disappointed shake of his head. "Shouldn't you have told her the truth?"

"I made a mistake. A big mistake. You just can't imagine the hell it is not knowing what the future holds, whether or not I'll just put Liz right back to where she was with Gramps. Liz shouldn't have to go through that a second time." Adam stated his fears out loud for the first time. "I need to know she's OK. I care about her. You know that."

"I know." Larry slapped his arm. "Like I said, you should have told her everything and let her decide for herself what she wanted for her future."

"But what if…?" What if she'd chosen to walk away?

Adam gulped. Was that why he'd put Liz through all this? Because he'd been afraid when push came to shove she'd leave him? Or had he been more afraid she wouldn't leave and he'd be forced to see the pain in her eyes when and if she was forced to take care of him?

"What if…?" Larry prompted.

"Nothing." Adam shook his head. "I believed I was doing the right thing. Stupid, I know, but being told you have MS does funny things to a person's ability to think clearly."

"Apparently." Larry sighed, glanced down the hallway at two nurses heading their way. "Look, we've been friends for a long time, and you know I have your best interests at heart. But Liz is my patient and I owe her certain courtesies—like respecting her wishes regarding visitors." Larry ran his fingers across his forehead. "We've all had a long day. Go home, get some rest. If

Liz wakes up, she's not going to be up to a confrontation with you. She needs rest. You need rest. I'm going to run the dynamic duo out of her room so she can get that rest." His gaze met Adam's. "I don't want you upsetting my patient. Or getting upset yourself. You can bend over backwards to make up with Liz when you're both more up to it."

"You want me to just leave her?"

"I promise I'll take good care of her for you, Adam."

"But what if she needs...?" He started to say "me", but hesitated. What if she needed him? If she did, would she even ask for him after everything that he'd said and done?

"You could sleep in the doctors' lounge," Larry suggested. "I'll wake you if there's any change or if she asks for you."

The doctors' lounge. Would there be any point? How could he possibly sleep after tonight's events?

"Or if I think she needs you," Larry added perceptively. "Rest, Adam. I can give you a mild sedative if you need something to take the edge off."

Adam shook his head. "Thanks for the offer, but I don't want to be drugged. Neither am I leaving the hospital. If Liz needs me, I want to be close."

Adam waited until he saw Liz's watch dragons leave her room, courtesy of Larry. He suspected Larry knew he was there, but his friend avoided looking in his direction and Adam appreciated that.

Knowing the glass walls that allowed the intensive care nurses to see Liz would also allow them to see him, he slipped into her room anyway.

He'd be quick, but if someone noticed they wouldn't think too much about him being in the room with her, wouldn't ask him to leave. Although people knew there were problems, they didn't know specifics of his and Liz's relationship. Not unless Liz had told them, and he doubted that.

He stood next to her hospital bed, soaking in the sight of the wires and attachments to her body. Her hair was pulled back from her face and he reached out to run his finger along the discolored skin beneath the sutured cut on her forehead.

In the dim light, she looked tiny, fragile, helpless. The beeping of her monitors pulsed around him like a living thing.

Her cheek felt silky smooth beneath his fingertip. As with any time he touched her, electricity sparked low in his gut.

Just as protectiveness also washed through him.

"Oh, Liz." If he could take on her pain, ease her suffering by taking it on himself, he would without batting an eyelash.

"What have I done to you?" He leaned over, breathed in her scent. Although mingled with the smell of cleansing antiseptic, the unique fragrance that was Liz filled him.

No matter how long he lived he'd never grow so old that he wouldn't recognize her scent. He imagined he'd close his eyes and dream of breathing her in, of touching her, kissing her, holding her, all the days of his life.

Selfish fool that he was, he wanted to be there for Liz. He always wanted to be there for her, a permanent part of her life.

So far his MS hadn't improved with the injections, but even that evening Dr Winters had said it was too early to tell.

What if Dr Winters was right? What if the exacerbation went away and he never had another flare-up of his MS? Or only a few throughout his lifetime without any long-term ill-effects?

He loved Liz. Loved her more than any other man possibly could.

Even if he had an acute flare-up, wouldn't them being together be better than her being with someone who could never love her as deeply as he did?

Or was that wishful thinking on his part?

Because Liz was easy to love and no doubt any number of men could fall madly in love with her. What wasn't to love about a kind, gentle-spirited beauty who gave so much of herself to those around her?

But what they had was strong, special. The kind of bond that spanned eternity and bound their souls together.

Which was why he'd done such a dismal job of setting Liz free. They belonged together.

If he did have acute flare-ups, he'd spend his good days making up to her for all the bad ones.

Liz. He laced his fingers with hers and lifted her hand to his mouth. He placed a gentle kiss on each finger.

"You deserve better, Liz. So much better than I am at my best, but if you'll have me I'll spend the rest of my life loving you and making up for these past few weeks."

CHAPTER NINE

"HELLO, May," Adam said to the woman he'd operated on the previous day. He'd spent the night at the hospital, waiting for news on Liz, hoping she'd send for him. She hadn't. To pass the long hours, he'd checked on May a couple of times. He'd ordered her another unit of packed RBCs, but otherwise she'd had a good night.

Adam couldn't say the same about his own night.

After sneaking into Liz's room a second time, just to make sure she was still OK, he'd lain down in an empty patient room for a couple of hours.

"Dr Cline." Although she was weak, May's lips turned up with pleasure when she spotted him. Her husband stood, rushed over to Adam.

"Dr Cline." He didn't say more, just shook Adam's hand over and over with great gusto, his eyes brimming with emotion.

Adam nodded in understanding, waited until May's husband stepped back, looking a little embarrassed.

"It's good to see you smiling," Adam told his patient, pleased with her skin color and the verve in her eyes.

Although still pale and a long way from being recovered, May was going to be OK.

"Just knowing that rock is out of me makes me want to smile."

"More like the root system of a tree than a rock." May's surgery was definitely the most complicated he'd ever undertaken. No doubt he'd be called before the board about his "collapse", but given the same set of circumstances he'd opt to do the surgery again. "A mighty oak's roots."

"Whatever." She shuddered. "I'm glad it's gone."

"We all are." Her husband sat back down next to her, placed his hand over his wife's.

"The nurse told me that you refused to take any pain medicine this morning."

"Why would I? My pain now is nothing compared to before you operated."

On cue the nurse walked into the room, handed Adam a printout of the most recent results on May's labs. "Thought you might want to see these, Dr Cline. I know you were asking about them earlier. They just got entered into the computer a few moments ago, so I printed out a copy."

Adam glanced over May's hemoglobin and hematocrit levels. Still low, but holding steady to what they had been after the infusion of her last blood transfusion. A good sign that she wasn't bleeding internally.

"Thanks, Kathy," he told the nurse.

"May has hurt for so long." Her husband took May's hand in his, brought it to his lips and placed a kiss on her pale skin. "Finally she can start looking forward to life again. For that, we'll always be grateful to you, Dr Cline."

"The outcome could have just as easily have been different," he reminded them, uncomfortable with the lavish praise.

Thank goodness May had no knowledge that her surgeon had completed the procedure with numb fingers. That he had sat down prior to her being stapled, that the vascular surgeon and the nephrologist had finished without him.

Thank goodness she didn't know her surgeon had temporarily gone blind in one eye.

He swallowed back the thoughts that memory brought with it.

Yesterday had been the worst day of his life in so many ways.

"Well, it didn't go differently and my family can never thank you enough," John said.

Awkward heat flooding his cheeks, Adam pulled back May's blanket and checked the large incision that ran from right beneath her sternum down to her pubis. The wound was holding together excellently with the staples Dr Robards had put in. There wasn't any sign of infection or bleeding. He hoped to keep it that way.

"Everything looks great. I'll come by and check you again this afternoon. The vascular surgeon and the nephrologist will both be by as well. Do as they say." He sighed, meeting May's expectant gaze. "I wish we'd been able to save your kidney, but it just wasn't possible. Dr Robards and Dr Nash are both excellent at their craft. Be assured they tried."

"I'm alive. I know you all did your best." May nodded her understanding. "Besides, losing a kidney is nothing compared to what you've given me, Dr Cline.

What you've all done for me. The fact you were able to remove the tumor is a miracle."

A miracle.

He was no miracle worker.

"Dr Robards and Dr Nash deserve credit for your surgery being so successful. Without them, yesterday wouldn't have happened."

The couple looked ready to argue, but Adam distracted them by asking the nurse about May's input via her IV, as she wasn't allowed to eat or drink yet, and her output from her catheter. He'd already looked at the record on the computer, knew the numbers were decent, but he needed a change of subject.

Adam spent a few more minutes speaking with the couple, leaving shortly after their daughter arrived and began gushing praise of her own.

May surviving the surgery had been a miracle, but not one at his hand.

Seeing May smile, her husband's and daughter's looks of relief and love made the all-day, stressful surgery worthwhile.

That evening Liz forced a smile to her face, hoping Kelly and Mona would quit clucking over her like mother hens. "Would you please sit down?"

Her friend kept pacing around the room, checking first one thing then another. With the way Kelly had gone over her room and equipment, Liz had every confidence each detail had been triple-checked.

She'd been transferred from Intensive Care that morning to a regular medical room. Not that she remembered. She didn't. Not from the moment her car had hit the deer then the tree until she'd woken up to see Mona dozing in the chair next to her bed that afternoon. But apparently she'd been awake off and on, spoken, interacted with her friends and coworkers last night and that morning.

"Sit down," she repeated, a bit more firmly.

"I can't. I'm on duty until seven," Kelly reminded.

"Other than aching like the devil, I'm fine. At least, I will be." Her gaze went to where her foot was propped upon a pillow. Apparently, she had three fractures in her right ankle. She wasn't exactly sure how she'd managed to accomplish that feat during the accident. A concussion, multiple contusions, two lacerations requiring sutures, and three fractures in her distal tibia.

Liz's fingers rested over her belly, just as it had done constantly since she'd woken up. "I have to talk to Dr Graviss."

"He's not going to let you go home yet so don't even bother asking," Kelly said so bossily Liz would have laughed had movement of any kind not hurt so much.

"Thanks, anyway, but I'm not ready to go home even if he would discharge me. I want my leg fixed first."

"I'll call for him," Kelly said, gave her a hug, then headed for the door. Before she left the room, Dr Graviss entered.

"What can I say? I'm that good." Kelly gave a whimsical smile, as if she'd summoned him with mystical powers, shrugged, and then followed the doctor over to Liz's bed.

"How's my favorite patient?" he asked.

"Stable," Kelly informed him, kicking into nurse mode. "Her last vitals were excellent."

Dr Graviss pulled up Liz's electronic chart and glanced over the information Kelly had entered earlier. When he'd finished, he turned and shook his head. "I was pleased to get Kelly's call this morning that you were back in the land of the living. You gave us quite a scare."

"I gave myself quite a scare," Liz admitted.

"You're banged up but, other than a few scars here and there, you should heal well." His gaze dropped to where her right ankle was propped. "Except for the fractures."

Liz looked at her bandaged leg. "How bad are the breaks?"

"Your distal tibia is going to have to be pinned together. Dr Bell will be by this evening. I suspect he'll schedule surgical correction within a couple of days if you're agreeable."

"What about my…?" She hesitated. "Pregnancy?"

Kelly and Mona exchanged looks, but neither appeared surprised. More as if from the moment she'd woken up they'd been waiting for her to tell them. She'd wanted to tell Adam first.

Dr Graviss looked nonplussed. "Best I can tell, no harm was done during the crash. It's fortunate that you're not far along as your body cushioned the impact. Everything should be fine with the baby." He glanced suspiciously at Mona and Kelly then his gaze met hers, as if he was wondering if they'd told her. "You knew?"

Her friends definitely had been waiting for her to say something. They must have wondered if she'd even known since she'd not told them.

"I knew." She started to nod, caught her breath at the

intense pain that shot through her at the movement, and spoke instead. "I saw an obstetrician yesterday."

Had it really only been yesterday afternoon that she'd gone to Dr Saunders? That felt like a lifetime ago.

"I'll get an ultrasound ordered. I ran the machine over you, but all I was checking was the baby's status."

"Everything looked normal?" Her hand still rested over her belly and she moved her fingers protectively.

"Everything looked wonderful. Your baby has a strong heartbeat, and you've not had any spotting. At this point, it's unlikely the accident will cause any complications." He gave a pointed look. "Just no stress allowed."

No stress. Right. Because she'd had none of that for weeks and weeks now.

"Discussing surgery on my ankle won't be stressful?"

He gave a wry smile. "I was referring to Adam. Does he know about the baby?"

"I haven't seen Adam since before the accident. That I recall, that is." Kelly and Mona had told her about him coming into the radiology room to check on her.

"He wants to see you, but I've forbidden him to come anywhere near you. Any more stress right now would be hard on you and on the baby. Until you feel up to it, I don't want Adam here."

A wave of loss washed over her. Dr Graviss had forbidden Adam to come near her? She supposed it made sense. She really didn't need more stress. Stress did bad things to a person. Could prevent her from healing. Could cost her precious things.

Her baby was OK. That's all that mattered right now. Everything else she'd deal with somehow. Just so long as she didn't lose Adam's baby. Everything else would work out. Maybe not as she'd hoped, how she'd dreamed, but she'd cope, find new dreams with her baby, and she'd count her blessings.

"Adam doesn't need the stress either," Dr Graviss continued. "He's got enough on his plate."

Liz stared at the doctor, knowing he knew more than she did. Lots more. "Tell me."

"The hospital board has summoned him for an emergency session." He hesitated long enough that Liz knew he wasn't telling her everything.

"Over May?" Liz moved, winced, but the pain didn't lessen her worry over her friend. "I was told she was doing OK."

"May is doing fantastically according to all accounts."

"Then why would the board even care any more?"

"Dr Mills didn't take kindly to Adam operating on May after he'd deemed her inoperable. Particularly as from all appearances the surgery was a success. Makes him look a bit incompetent to have ruled her inoperable."

"Arrogant bastard," Kelly interjected from where she stood at the foot of Liz's bed.

"His father has been on the board for over twenty years," Mona added unnecessarily. They all knew Dr Mills's father decided every move the board made.

Dr Graviss shrugged. "Adam did the right thing, but I understand the board's take. Operating on May was a liability."

"Doctors do things like that every day," Liz reminded him. "Every patient that's operated on is at risk. The hospital board should stay out of it."

Dr Graviss smiled at Liz's adamant stance. "Since they're responsible for procedures done in this facility—"

"I know," she interrupted softly. "You're right, of course. But, well, we all wanted to believe May didn't have to go on in such pain, just waiting to die. No one should have to suffer that way." She closed her eyes, memories washing over her. "Or to watch someone they love suffer that way."

"Feel strongly about this, do you?"

"Of course." Liz yawned, as exhaustion swept over her. "Adam gave May back hope."

"He's a good doctor," Dr Graviss agreed. "A good man. Misguided at times, but always trying to do what he thinks is the right thing."

Liz felt like the doctor was trying to tell her something significant. She closed her eyes, intent on studying what that something might be, but despite the three people in her hospital room she fell asleep.

Flustered by his latest round with the hospital board, Adam checked on an appendectomy patient and a cholecystectomy patient he'd operated on that morning. Both were doing well and he'd written discharge orders. Despite every intention to quickly leave that floor, he lingered outside Liz's hospital room.

How was she? Not that he wasn't keeping tabs on her. But Larry only told him so much and the man had forbidden him to go anywhere near Liz today. Did he think he was going to demand she give him a second chance whether she wanted to or not?

He'd also consulted with Dr Bell on Liz's ankle and the orthopedic surgeon planned to operate next morning.

Was Liz dreading surgery? Looking forward to getting her ankle repaired? *Had she forgiven him for ruining her life?*

He'd like to see her, but now that she'd regained consciousness sneaking in wouldn't be a simple matter of walking into the room. He couldn't risk upsetting her, causing her stress of any kind. Larry had strictly warned him that to do so would be detrimental to Liz's progress.

Soon, though, he would tell Liz everything that was in his heart. He'd tell her how much he missed her. How much he longed for the days when he'd been able to hold her in his arms to his heart's content and he'd do anything to have those days back, to have the opportunity to make up to her for his foolishness.

She'd asked him to leave the last time she'd seen him.

Surely that had only been shock setting in and she hadn't meant she didn't want him near her.

Which was what he kept telling himself the next day as he sauntered through the hospital hallway at four in the morning.

It didn't surprise him to find Liz sleeping. He should be sleeping, too, since he was supposed to be getting rest, but he'd been unable to sleep and had opted to come in to the hospital.

Adam stood by Liz's bed, watching her chest rise and fall, watching the flicker of her eyes as she dreamed. Although at first glance she appeared to be resting peacefully, she moaned and despite the risk of her waking he laced his fingers through hers, clasping her hand.

As before, seeing Liz banged up from her accident brought fresh waves of helplessness, loss, guilt. Her crash had been an accident, but he'd never forgive himself for the role he'd inadvertently played.

"My sweet, sweet Liz." He lifted her hand to his mouth and kissed the soft skin.

A noise from the other side of the room had him turning. An elderly lady lay sleeping in the hospital bed next to hers.

The sight of Liz had distracted him so completely that he'd failed to notice her new roommate. From the traction equipment, she'd obviously broken her hip and was probably in a well-medicated sleep. Thank goodness, as he'd been oblivious to everything but Liz.

Still holding her hand, Adam stood over Liz's bed, watching her breathe, wishing he could take away all her pain, wishing he could have been the one behind the wheel of her car since his future held nothing but shadows.

CHAPTER TEN

SEVERAL days following her surgery, Liz struggled to sit up in her hospital bed without jarring her ankle. Dr Bell had performed surgery and placed metal pins inside her ankle to clasp the tibia bone back into one piece. He'd said that with rest, physical therapy, and determination, she should be back to work in a couple of months. Maybe sooner.

A couple of months.

However was she going to survive financially, being out of work that long?

She couldn't afford to be laid up. Between the hospital stay and the follow-up, she'd be digging a hole much deeper than the one she'd been buried in.

Since burdening Adam with her debts was no longer an issue, she shouldn't stress so much, but now there was a baby to consider. A baby she'd need to take time off work to have and to recover from having, a baby she wanted time to bond with. There would be lots of new expenses like more medical bills, diapers, and childcare.

Her heart squeezed at the thought she'd have to leave

her baby in someone else's care so she could return to work as soon as physically possible.

Once he learned of their baby, Adam would insist on helping financially regardless of how he felt about her and the baby. But she balked at the idea of accepting money from him.

She missed him, wanted to talk with him to tell him about their baby, but it wasn't as if she could chase him down, not with her ankle, and he hadn't been to see her.

If he'd really wanted to see her he would have come regardless of Dr Graviss's warning not to. She supposed Dr Graviss ordering him to stay away had seemed like a godsend to Adam. Perhaps the doctor had done so as a favor to his friend.

Single, pregnant, and ignored by the man she cared most for. Perhaps she should hate him.

No matter what was going on in their relationship, Dr Graviss was right. Adam was a good man. She'd spent too much time with him to believe otherwise. Even if things truly were over between them, she'd never regret the time they'd shared.

He'd given her the strength to face each day with a smile during the hardest days of Gramps's illness. Given her hope that tomorrow would be a better day.

Of course, she'd always believed her tomorrows would hold Adam.

"You sure are lost in thought, dearie." Nannie Robbins's sweet grandmotherly voice interrupted from the other side of the hospital room. Due to the hospital being full up, Liz had lost her private room and was now in the company of an elderly lady who'd fallen and broken her hip.

"I was thinking about life," Liz admitted, wondering how Nannie's cheery disposition never seemed to fade. She had to be in intense pain, yet she'd not voiced a single complaint.

The older woman nodded as if she knew exactly what Liz's thoughts had been. "Yes, life's the most precious gift we have."

Liz wouldn't argue. Her body contained that precious gift, a tiny new person she and Adam had created. For that she would always be grateful.

"When all is said and done, life and love is really all that matters," Nannie continued with the wisdom of her eighty-plus years of life experience.

"Yes." Life and love. It sounded simple. "Yet it's so easy to get caught up in the everyday things that pull us down. To forget just how blessed we are."

With Gramps's illness and death, then the problems with Adam, she'd forgotten. Forgotten all the wonderful things in her life, like her friends, the job she loved, her health. She'd had much to be thankful for even before she'd learned about her pregnancy.

"True," Nannie said, and Liz got the feeling that if the woman could have reached her, she'd have patted her hand. "Nothing should pull you down, dearie, not so long as you have life and love. Love is your shield, life your sword. Use them to guide you through this world and to protect you from sorrows."

Liz blinked, thinking she'd somehow missed out on part of the conversation. Or that Nannie really was a mind reader.

"Is Adam who you're in love with?"

Liz's gaze shot to the crinkly-faced, smiling woman.

Not once since Nannie had been moved into her room had Liz mentioned Adam. Not once. "Why would you ask that?"

"Because you cried for him last night in your sleep. You must love him a great deal to miss him so."

Liz winced. She'd dreamed about Adam last night, dreamed about how he'd been able to make her laugh no matter how down she'd been, how he'd known just what to say to bring a smile to her face, how she'd felt safe, content when he'd held her. "I'm sorry. I didn't mean to disturb you."

"No disturbance, dearie," Nannie assured her.

"I'll try not to bother you tonight."

"No bother," the woman said brightly. So brightly Liz wondered what kind of meds Nannie's IV was delivering. "As I said, love is a beautiful thing. Especially true love."

True love. Her heart twisted in her chest.

"Love can also be cruel when it's unrequited," she said so softly she was surprised when Nannie's white brows rose.

"Your Adam doesn't love you?"

Once upon a time she'd believed with her whole heart that Adam loved her. She'd been a naïve, trusting fool. "No, he doesn't love me."

"You're sure?"

"Positive."

An odd look passed over Nannie's face and for a moment her smile slipped, then her expression brightened again. "Tell me about this man who has your heart."

Tell her about Adam? She'd rather not talk about him. Not think about him.

"Tell me when you first knew you loved him," the woman encouraged, a far-away look lighting her eyes. "There's nothing more healing than new love."

When had she first known she loved Adam?

She'd really like to just ignore Nannie's request, feign tiredness, and get lost in her own thoughts. But the woman looked so wistful, so expectant, Liz didn't have the heart.

"It's nothing terribly romantic," she warned, just in case Nannie was expecting something straight out of a romance novel.

"Love is always romantic when one looks through the eyes of the lover. Never forget that."

Liz eyed the older lady with renewed wonder. Nannie's face glowed with excitement. Talking with the cheery woman made something inside Liz not hurt quite so much, so she smiled in return.

"My grandfather was ill for a very long time," she began. "I lived with him from the time I was a little girl, and after he got sick I provided his evening and night care. His doctor had told me only the day before that he wouldn't live much longer and to be prepared."

She'd not wanted to believe, had refused to believe she was going to lose him.

"Gramps had a particularly rough night, and I was too tense to sleep." She'd sat vigil over his bed, praying, crying, assessing vitals, praying some more. "By morning, I was wound tighter than a spring."

"Go on," Nannie encouraged with a wink. "Get to the good stuff."

Liz grinned at her impatience. "From the beginning of our relationship Adam understood that we couldn't date like a normal couple. On this particular occasion we'd made plans to spend the day together for Adam's birthday. I'd bought tickets to a show in Jackson. We were going to drive up and spend the day just being together."

She'd wanted to give him one day of being a regular couple, a day where he took precedence in her life. Like so many things in their relationship, the day hadn't gone according to plan.

"When Adam picked me up that morning, he took one look, drove me to his place instead, and insisted I take a nap before we headed out."

He'd tucked her into his bed like she'd been a small child, complete with a kiss on the forehead. God, he'd been sweet, telling her he'd man her cellphone. If anything happened with her grandfather, he'd wake her.

"I slept for seven hours and we missed the show. I felt so bad, but he wasn't upset. Instead, he ran me a bath and cooked dinner." He'd made her spaghetti. Even now the delicious aroma drifted through her mind, making her mouth water. "While we were eating, I realized I'd been laughing, that I felt happy inside, light, like I could go home to Gramps and give him my love without shedding tears."

Time with Adam had kept her spirits lifted during the darkest days. Her keeping a positive outlook had to have made a difference to Gramps, had to have helped ease his suffering.

She protectively placed her hand over her abdomen, allowing past emotions to wash over her afresh.

"I looked up to tell Adam how much I appreciated his ability to make me feel whole, warm, alive, and…" her throat tightened, her voice choked "…I saw the same warmth in his eyes."

He'd looked at her as if she was his whole reason for existing.

"In that moment, the world seemed perfect, and I knew my heart belonged to him and always would."

Nannie gave a heartfelt sigh.

Liz smiled sheepishly. "Not what you were expecting to hear, I imagine. Nothing flowery or overly romantic. Just him setting aside our plans for his special day to put my needs first." Heat burned her cheeks. "He told me that being with me was the best birthday present he'd ever received."

She'd thought his words the most romantic she'd ever heard.

For those few hours that evening it had just been her and Adam and life had felt perfect.

"A beautiful love story," Nannie said with obvious appreciation. "Reminds me of me and my Edward."

"Tell me," Liz asked, sensing Nannie wanted her turn. "Tell me when you knew you loved your Edward."

With a far-away look on her face, the woman launched into a tale of young love, causing Liz to forget everything but the woman's words.

For the next hour Nannie told her all about her marriage to the man of her dreams. A man who'd never returned from the war he'd fought for his country so many years ago.

"Oh, Nannie, I'm so sorry."

The older woman's forehead creased. "Why, dearie? Edward and I shared love. Whether we'd had one week together or a lifetime, what we had was real. That's what counts."

Liz fought tears. "You're a very special person, Nannie. A very wise person."

Nannie nodded with a supremely knowing look on her face. "When you're as old as I am, you've learned a thing or two."

"What are you ladies up to?" Dr Bell asked, flashing a mouthful of bright whites as he entered their room. He gave Nannie a special just-for-her wink, checked her hip, and administered a dose of the morphine pump she never seemed to remember to give herself. When Nannie was settled, he turned to Liz. "How's the leg?"

She forced a smile and gestured to where her leg was in traction. "Just hanging around."

"Nice one." He grinned, examining her toes, which were sticking out of the air cast on her foot and ankle. He lightly pinched each one over the nail bed, watching to see how quickly the color came back. The pink color returned instantaneously. "Good capillary refill. Excellent."

"Are you going to let me go home yet?" she asked, wondering how she'd manage to care for herself but knowing she'd find a way. If Dr Bell refused to let her hobble on crutches, she'd see about borrowing a wheelchair from the hospital.

"What?" he teased while he checked the tightness of her air cast. "You're not loving our hospitality?"

"Do you want the truth?"

He laughed. "That bad, huh?"

"Although having Nannie in my room has helped, I'm going stir crazy." Which was the truth. Kelly and Mona had brought some novels and magazines, but she could only read for short periods of time or she got a severe headache. Something she hoped would pass soon. Most of the time she just lay in bed with her palms over her belly, thinking about Adam, their baby, what might have gone wrong, and what she was going to do about the future. Until today, Nannie had slept most of the time. Then again, so had she.

"Have you seen Adam?" she asked before she could censor herself.

Dr Bell's smile slipped. "He's not been by?"

The guilty look on his face said he knew more than he was letting on.

"No. Has Dr Graviss lifted the ban?"

Dr Bell didn't meet her gaze, just making a show of checking what he'd already checked. "I ran into him last night."

"And?"

He took a while to answer.

"Honestly? May's surgery got to him. He looked like hell. Whatever happened between the two of you in the past, Adam needs you." Glancing at Nannie's sleeping form first, he whispered, "You have to tell him about the baby. He deserves to know."

Adam needed her? Then why had he pushed her away? Liz closed her eyes, steadied herself, and met the orthopedic surgeon's gaze with annoyance. "How do you know I haven't told him?"

"Because he's listened to Larry's order to stay away until you're stronger. If he knew you were pregnant, neither hell nor high water would keep him away."

"Do you think knowing about our baby will change his mind about me? That knowing I'm pregnant will make him want me again?" Days of pent-up frustration and doubt came to a head inside her. "Let me ask you something. If Adam did change his mind, if he did want to be here with me, would you want a man who was only with you because you were pregnant?"

"No," Dr Bell answered. "But you and I both know there's more between you and Adam than just a pregnancy."

She sighed. "I thought so, too, once, but now…"

"Now?"

"I'm not sure." She rubbed her right temple. "When I think over our relationship I can see I was so blinded by love for Adam and by caring for Gramps that I didn't see the truth. That I was just another woman in his life."

"You don't believe that. The fact you're pregnant makes you more than just another woman in his life."

She gave an ironic laugh. "I don't think he'll be thrilled that I'm pregnant."

"Talk to him and let him decide for himself how he feels about the baby. About you."

"Don't you think the fact he's not been to see me says exactly how he feels?"

His face pinched with thought. "Yes, it does. He cares enough that when Larry told him to stay away to protect your health and well-being, he's done his best to do just that."

"It's been almost a week. Any danger I was in passed long ago. He could have stopped by."

Dr Bell ran his finger down the edge of her air cast. "He's been by."

Liz scooted up, swatting his hand away from her leg. "What? Adam's been by? When?"

"He's come by to see you on several occasions. You just weren't awake."

"How do you know that?"

He shrugged. "Word gets around."

"Someone told you Adam came to see me?"

"Actually, Nannie mentioned you'd been having company."

"Nannie?" Liz glanced over at the sleeping woman she'd grown fond of over the past few days. "She saw Adam here? She never said anything to me." Liz scowled. "Why would she tell you?"

He shrugged. "She wanted to know if Adam was your baby's father and whether or not she should toss him out next time he came by."

Although it was silly since she'd only known the woman for a few days, Liz felt twinges of guilt that she'd not told Nannie she was pregnant. Apparently Nannie had worked it out for herself.

"With the way news travels around this place, I guess there are a lot of people who know," Liz mused. Did Adam? Was that why he'd come to her room?

Dr Bell crossed his arms. "You'd be surprised at how few people know."

"That I'm pregnant?"

"There's a few who've found out, but mostly it's hush-hush, Liz. For obvious reasons, I've been discreet with who can access your records. So has Larry. Adam doesn't know, if that's what you're wondering." He touched her arm. "Don't you think it's time he did?"

"Dr Cline," Adam's office nurse said when he came out of the exam room where he'd been removing a lipoma from a forty-two-year-old's back. "You have company in your office. Your next appointment isn't for another thirty minutes so there's no rush."

She smiled overly brightly and gave him a wink. Immediately Adam guessed who waited in his office. Liz.

Ignoring his nurse's knowing look, he paused only long enough to rake his fingers through his hair before going into his office.

She sat in a wheelchair with her back to him. Her right leg was elevated on an attached foot rest and she wore a feminine housecoat he'd never seen before. Probably a gift from one of her friends.

She looked beautiful. A sight for sore eyes. His heart rate quickened. She hadn't moved to indicate she realized he was there, but instinctively he knew she was aware of him.

The awareness pulsed between them like a living beat drawing him under its spell.

Liz. Liz. Liz. His heart thrummed.

But he couldn't speak.

As time ticked between them, she turned the wheelchair to face him. Her movements weren't smooth, but weren't too bad considering today was probably the first time she'd used it. At least, Larry hadn't mentioned Liz having outings. And although Adam's office was technically a part of the hospital, the general surgery ambulatory clinic was quite a trek from the medical floor.

Liz in a wheelchair.

She would recover, he knew that, but the sight of her condition hit him badly.

Her gaze met his and he saw a thousand emotions dancing in the depths of her eyes.

"Adam."

His name sounded sweet on her lips, but she didn't mean it as an endearment. More like a well-deserved reprimand.

"We need to talk."

"The last time we talked didn't end so well." He gestured to her wheelchair.

"My accident had nothing to do with our 'talk'. Yes, I was upset when I crashed, but that deer didn't know my world had fallen to bits."

"I'm sorry, Liz," he automatically apologized, trying to figure out where to start on winning Liz's forgiveness. On putting the bits of her world back together in a way where they could find happiness again.

"Before we get into why I'm here, Adam, thank you for what you did for May. I stopped by her hospital room to see her and she looks wonderful. Thank you."

Pride filled him at Liz's praise. He'd been given hell from the board, but seeing the pride in Liz's eyes gave him the stamina to face ten boards. God, he'd missed her.

If he hadn't thought she'd slap him, he'd take her in his arms and kiss her until she was breathless.

She rolled her wheelchair past him and after a few jerky movements closed the door. Not a loud slam, just a quiet catching of the latch. "Sit down."

Watching her in the wheelchair left him immobile, weak-kneed. Her strength of will amazed him, left him a little in awe of her. He had more than a sneaking suspicion that had their situations been reversed, Liz would have faced a diagnosis of MS head on rather than trying to withdraw from life.

He'd been such a fool.

A well-intentioned fool, but a fool all the same.

"Sit down,' she repeated, her voice terse. "I don't want you towering over me, and I can't stand up. Yet."

Adam crossed his arms and bit back a smile. Seeing her spunk did his heart good. She really was getting better, would heal and get her life back. Her strength would push him, help him be a better man, would force him to fight his MS and win.

Could she forgive him?

"I came to tell you on the night I had the crash but…" She compressed her lips a moment. "Well, things didn't go as I'd hoped. Telling you in the middle of the day while you're at work isn't ideal, but you need to know, before you find out from someone else," she continued, gripping the armrests of her wheelchair until her knuckles whitened. "So here I am."

He quirked an eyebrow, trying to figure out what she was talking about, wondering how he was going to ask her to love a man who had an iffy future, to give him a second chance and overlook these past few weeks.

How did you tell someone that you'd felt like you'd been given a death sentence and didn't want to drag them down, too? That you'd forgotten that it wasn't the quantity but the quality that defined a person's life?

"I'm pregnant."

Pregnant?

God, no. He couldn't have heard Liz correctly.

He sat down, realizing too late that he wasn't as close to his desk as he'd thought and slipped, regaining his balance only in the nick of time to keep from falling. Not a smooth move, but he was so shaken inside he wasn't sure he'd recognize smooth if it whacked him across the face.

"What did you say?" Please, don't let him have made Liz pregnant. Not when any baby he gave her would carry his defective genes.

Her lower lip disappeared between her teeth, but her gaze remained locked with his. "I'm pregnant, Adam."

The vein at his temple threatened to burst open. Nausea tore at his gag reflex. "How?"

"How?" She gave him a confused look. "You know *how*."

"It's mine?" Of course Liz's baby would be his, but she'd be so much better off if it weren't. God, he wished it weren't.

Last night, when he'd considered winning Liz's forgiveness, he'd thought about the future. In his mind he'd thought they could adopt or have artificial insemination from a healthy donor. Never in any of his wildest dreams of begging Liz to forgive him had he considered making her pregnant. Never.

"I'm not going to dignify your question with an answer." She glared at him. "Coming here was a mistake. But I had to tell you about our baby." Her hands shook. "From your reaction I…well, just know that I don't expect anything from you. I just thought you should know."

"How far along are you?"

She paused, scraped her fingernail over the rubber coating on the wheelchair's armrest. "According to the ultrasound Dr Graviss ran, I'm fourteen weeks."

"Fourteen weeks." There was no mistaking the look of relief on his face. "That's not too late for an abortion."

His heart ached at the thought, but there would be other babies. Babies conceived through artificial insemination. Babies who wouldn't be at high risk of developing MS.

Fourteen weeks. He thought back to when that would have been. Fourteen weeks ago he'd made love to Liz and put his baby in her belly.

They'd always used a condom. Always. But he did recall one afternoon. Gramps had had a rough night and they'd thought he wouldn't pull through, but somehow he had yet again managed to hang on. Hospice had come on schedule and he'd whisked an unsure Liz to his place to get a few hours' rest and relaxation. Instead, they'd made love, clinging to each other for reaffirmation of life after a night of battling death for a beloved grandfather. They'd used a condom, but when he'd taken it off it had torn.

Or maybe it had already been torn?

Oh, hell. How could he have been so irresponsible as to start a baby when he stood a chance of passing on a horrible disease to an innocent child? Liz's child.

His gaze met Liz's and he saw the horrendous hurt in her glassy eyes.

"You bastard." She slid her fingers until she connected with the wheels. Moving back to the door, she leaned forward. Although it took a couple of tries, she maneuvered the wheelchair to where she opened the door and rolled out.

Stunned, Adam watched her disappear from his office.

Emotions he couldn't begin to identify swelled in his chest and pushed him into motion. He ran after her, catching up just as she thanked one of his patients for opening the door to let her out to the main hospital hallway. Kelly waited impatiently, tapping her foot and glaring at Adam.

"Liz?" He grabbed hold of the handle of her chair, stopping her progress because she either hadn't seen him or hadn't cared to stop if she had.

She didn't speak, didn't even look up at him, just stared straight ahead.

"What does this mean?" he asked.

Her forehead wrinkled and her gaze lifted. "What do you mean, what does this mean?"

What did he mean?

"For us?"

"Did you forget?" Her eyes turned cold, colder than he'd ever seen Liz, colder than he would have thought possible from Liz. She rolled free of his stunned grasp. "There is no us."

CHAPTER ELEVEN

ANY hope or belief in Adam shriveled up and died the moment he suggested an abortion.

The look on his face when she'd told him about their baby would haunt Liz all the days of her life.

He'd looked horrified.

Like he might throw up. Or pass out. Or just keel over with disgust.

He wanted her to have an abortion!

She wasn't able to prevent the whimper that escaped. Not in any of the scenarios she'd considered had she imagined Adam would want her to not have their baby.

Sure, abortion might be right for some, but not for her. Not when she so desperately wanted this baby.

Damn him for saying that. She'd thought she could forgive him anything. She'd just discovered that wasn't true.

"I can't believe him," Kelly huffed from where she walked next to the wheelchair.

Her friend had wanted to push her, but Liz needed to

expend the energy, work off the torrent coursing through her weakened body, feel in control of at least something in her life.

"He's done a total turn-around," Kelly continued. "Do you think he's on drugs?"

"Drugs? Adam?" Startled, Liz blinked up at her friend. "Adam doesn't do drugs."

"Well, he sure is acting weird. Up until Gramps died, the man was perfect. Every woman in the hospital was jealous of you. He adored you, and it was plain for everyone to see. Now he's just like every other man. A jerk."

At the moment she wouldn't argue with Kelly's assessment. Only a jerk would go green while being told he was going to be a father. Adam had gone a pale, putrid green.

"He is a jerk," Liz agreed.

"I could punch him in the face for you," Kelly offered.

"No." Liz shook her head. Admittedly, she'd felt like smacking him, but even if she'd been on her own two feet and capable, she doubted she would have. She wasn't a physically violent kind of person.

Although when he'd asked if their baby was his she had wanted to kick him. Hard.

How could he have asked her that?

Even now her fists clenched at his having done so.

Fourteen weeks. That's not too late for an abortion.

How dared he? Maybe she was more physically violent than she'd thought. Liz dry-heaved so violently she was unable to hide it from her friend.

Kelly placed her hand on Liz's shoulder. "Oh, Liz. Let's get you back to your room."

Liz covered her mouth, fighting another wave of disgust. Adam wanted her to destroy the life they'd made.

How could he not want their baby?

Not wanting her was one thing, but their baby?

Their baby.

Anger gurgled inside her.

Anger at the insensitive way he'd shut her out of his life.

Anger at her own stupidity for allowing it to happen.

Anger that he'd be so callous, so cold as to not want a baby he'd fathered.

Their baby was a miracle. A blessing. A gift.

How dared he?

Even if he got over the initial shock, accustomed himself to the idea of their baby, she'd never forget the look on his face. Never forgive that look. That show of true emotion.

She'd always know.

If Adam had his way, their baby would never enter the world.

"That's it," Kelly swore when she saw Liz's angry tears and misinterpreted them. "I'm going to punch him whether you want me to or not."

Kelly made a ka-pow motion that drew a strangled sound from Liz's throat.

"If that would solve anything, I'd say go for it."

"Hitting him would make me feel better," Kelly pointed out.

Liz actually considered it a moment, then wiped her eyes. Life was short and regardless of Adam she had a lot to live for, a lot to be happy about. No longer would she give him control over her emotions, over her heart. She and Adam were finished. Not because of him shutting her out, but finished because she was done with him.

"Don't bother," she advised her friend, and meant it. "He's not worth the effort."

Adam had numbly seen the rest of his afternoon patients. Despite his reduced schedule, he'd even performed an emergency appendectomy. But only because he could go through the motions without thought. Without acknowledging that he was stunned. Horrified. Ashamed.

Finished for the day, he rested his elbows on his desk and dropped his face into his tingling hands.

Liz was going to have a baby.

His baby.

Liz, who was the most wonderful woman he'd ever met, who was the woman he loved, was going to have his baby.

Elation battled horror.

From the moment he'd been diagnosed with MS, he'd known he'd never father any children. He'd planned to have a vasectomy soon after finishing his MS treatments to ensure he wouldn't.

How the hell could he have known he'd already fathered a baby?

How could he have a child when he'd only be condemning a child to battle with a disease that had the power to demand everything?

To have loved her, never wanted to hurt her, to keep from being a burden to her, he sure was doing a great job on Liz.

First his withdrawal following his diagnosis.

And now this.

He'd given her baby his genetically screwed-up genes.

Had she known about her pregnancy before the crash?

Of course she had. She'd said she had come to his condo to tell him that night. She had even mentioned a family, but he'd thought she'd meant a future family. Not one they'd already started.

He'd told her he didn't love her on the night she'd intended to tell him about their baby.

No wonder Liz had called him names. He was a bastard.

Fourteen weeks. That meant in twenty-six weeks he and Liz were going to be parents because from the way she'd looked at him he knew she wouldn't consider an abortion.

Liz was going to be a single mother, raising a baby on her own. A baby who could come down with MS, could require Liz to provide twenty-four-hour assistance, just like Gramps.

Any guilt he'd felt up to that point was as nothing in comparison to what flowed through him at the thought of what he'd done.

In his mind he'd had a clear idea of what the right thing was—for him to set Liz free.

Seeing her unconscious, having battled the thoughts that her life might be snuffed out, he'd realized he had to tell her about his MS, had to tell her he loved her, wanted her in his life. Like Larry had suggested, he'd planned to let Liz decide if she wanted to take that risk rather than him making all the decisions based on some misguided selflessness. *Selflessness.* He'd failed miserably.

Her pregnancy changed everything.

He should have told her about his MS before blurting out that it wasn't too late for an abortion.

He'd been in such shock, he hadn't been able to think straight. Had only known that he'd fouled up Liz's life in yet another way and he wanted to start getting things right.

Liz was pregnant with a baby who carried the potential to have MS. She was in a wheelchair. She probably hated him. All of it was his fault. If not for him, she'd be free for the first time in her life. Instead, she was going to go from caring for her grandfather to recovering from her own injuries to caring for a baby. A baby that she might be caring for for an entire lifetime.

She'd need him more than ever. To help her recover from her injuries and then to take care of her following the baby's arrival, to help her financially, to help her if their son or daughter came down with MS. If he stayed healthy himself.

Oh, hell.

What had he done?

It was only eight-thirty, but Liz lay in her hospital bed with her eyes closed.

All evening she'd put on a smile for her friends, given Dr Graviss and Dr Bell all the right answers when they'd checked on her. The only time her smile wavered was when Nannie's transfer papers came through and the older woman was relocated to a skilled nursing home. After Nannie's departure she'd feigned tiredness because the pretense had been too much.

The tiredness really hadn't been feigned so much as exaggerated. She was tired. Not that she could go to sleep. No, her mind was too wound up for that, her heart too twisted.

Just as she'd been able to tell, without turning, when Adam had entered his office, she became aware of him in her room without opening her eyes. He didn't make a sound, but all the same she knew he was there.

She could feel him. His strong presence sucked all the oxygen out of the room and left her light-headed.

What was he doing there?

Hadn't he done a good enough job ripping her heart out earlier in his office?

Fourteen weeks. That's not too late for an abortion.

He stood beside her bed, presumably watching her, and although it was wrong, she just lay there.

"Are you so upset with me you refuse to look at me?"

He had no idea. If she had to look at him she might spit in his handsome face. Or scratch his eyeballs out. Angry heat infused her face, but she still didn't open her eyes.

"Not that I blame you," he added, sounding just as tired as she'd felt moments before he'd entered her room. "But what you told me this afternoon shocked me, and I reacted badly. Everything I said came out wrong."

Reluctantly she opened her eyes, but she didn't speak. What could she say? Everything he'd said had come out wrong.

"You aren't going to make this easy, are you?"

She snorted. "Can you tell me a reason why I should?"

"Not a single one," he said solemnly.

"Finally something we agree on."

"You're pregnant, Liz."

She stared blankly at him, waiting for him to elaborate since he wasn't telling her anything she hadn't already known.

"I had no intention of fathering a child. Ever."

Ouch. "Sorry to disappoint you."

"I'm not disappointed." He stopped, raked his hand through his hair. "Or I wouldn't be if things were different."

Meaning if he loved her, if he'd wanted a future with her.

"Well, tough, because I'm not having an abortion and you'll just have to deal with it." She sucked in a deep breath, wincing from the stretching of her sore rib muscles. "I don't want anything from you, Adam. Go away."

"You need my help."

She gritted her teeth. Did he think her helpless? "I've got a good job. I'll get by."

"You're in a wheelchair."

"So? Until I get on my feet, I'll work a desk job. Lots of people are in wheelchairs and they get by just fine."

"A desk job?" He shook his head. "You aren't thinking straight, Liz. Yet another thing that's my fault. How could you when you don't have all the facts?"

Adam's look of torment did little to endear him to her. He truly found the idea of her being pregnant with his baby horrific. "All the facts? What facts?"

He paced across the small stretch separating her bed and the one Nannie had occupied. "Liz, a week or two before Gramps died, I started having…problems."

"Problems?" Dear Lord, had Kelly been right? Was Adam on drugs? She couldn't wrap herself around the notion no matter how hard she tried.

"Headaches. Mostly in my right temple. My vision got blurry on and off. Still does."

Liz's anger melted away in a single heartbeat, to be replaced with fear. Hadn't she thought something was wrong with Adam?

"I kept ignoring it, thinking I was just tired, stressed, had a virus. I can't even remember all the excuses I gave myself. The truth was, in my heart I knew something more was going on."

Liz's fear escalated. She stared at him, waiting for him to continue with what was sure to be a horror story.

"When my hands went numb I couldn't ignore what was going on any longer and I saw Larry, uh, Dr Graviss."

Liz's gaze dropped to where Adam clenched his fingers. He released them in a slow, exaggerated movement.

"I expected him to write a prescription for migraines. Tell me I'd been under too much stress. Maybe check me for diabetes. Imagine my surprise when he said he was referring me to a neurologist."

Liz bit the inside of her lip.

He slid his fingers into his pants pockets and looked directly into her eyes. "I have MS, Liz."

"No," Liz gasped. Adam had MS? It couldn't be true, but there was no denying the truth written on his face. "Oh, Adam."

He'd been dealing with all this and hadn't told her?

"You missed out on so much by caring for Gramps all that time, Liz." He made taking care of her grand-father sound like a prison sentence. "I just couldn't see continuing our relationship when it meant possibly putting you back in that position."

"That's insane. You sound like I had to be with Gramps, that caring for him wasn't my choice." She scooted up in her bed, biting back the need to wince at the pain the movement caused. "It was my choice, Adam. At all times I chose to care for Gramps, to keep him at home, because it's what he wanted and it was the right thing. But if you want to know the truth, it was mostly because I wanted every second with him. The time I had with Gramps meant more to me than anything."

"I know that now, Liz, but when this started I was grieving just as much as you. Grieving for my health, for the future I'd wanted for us, grieving because of what I believed was the right thing—ending our relationship because I knew you'd never walk away from me if you knew I was ill."

"I can't believe you were going through all this and didn't tell me. That you'd let me think I'd done something wrong after Gramps's funeral." She closed her eyes, counted to ten. She'd believed they loved each other, trusted each other. She'd been so wrong. He hadn't believed in her, hadn't trusted her. He'd kept the knowledge he had MS from her. "How could you be so selfish?"

"Selfish?" he asked, his brows drawing together. "I was trying to be selfless, Liz. To give you up so you wouldn't have to go through this hell with me."

"This hell? You look just fine to me."

"I went blind in my right eye on the day I performed May Probst's surgery," he blurted out.

"Blind?" Liz said in horror.

"Completely black. I collapsed onto the OR floor. The hospital board slapped my hands for my unprofessional conduct, threatened me with probation if anything of the kind ever happens again." He snorted. "Just wait until they find out about my MS."

"They don't know? You've been operating on people with numb hands, blind, and the board doesn't know?"

"The numbness comes and goes," he said defensively. "And there's only been the one episode of blindness and I'd finished my portion of May's surgery."

The enormity of what he was saying hit her. Adam could lose his career as a surgeon.

"Now you see why you have to have an abortion."

Liz stared at him in confusion. "What? I don't see that at all."

"I have MS, Liz. That means any child I have has a three to five percent increased chance of developing MS."

"I'm not having an abortion." If he'd said the odds were one hundred percent, she wouldn't abort his baby.

"Liz, once again you're not thinking straight. You can go and be artificially inseminated. There's no reason to take this chance."

"Do you realize what you're saying, Adam?" Despite her aching muscles, she shook her head. "By your own standards, you wouldn't be here, wouldn't have been born."

His jaw clenched. "You'd be a lot better off if that were the case."

"I'm not the one who's not thinking straight. Adam, MS isn't a death sentence. I've cared for patients with MS. Most lead wonderfully normal lives."

"What about the ones who don't?"

"How did I miss what an optimist you are?" she asked sarcastically.

"The same way you missed all my symptoms," he shot back.

"I…"

He shook his head, visibly remorseful. "Don't bother, Liz. That was a low blow on my part. I know the reasons why. They were the same reasons why I didn't tell you what was going on. Why I did my best to hide what was going on from you."

"I thought I told you to stay away from my patient because I didn't want her upset."

Liz and Adam both glanced toward the door. Dr Graviss stood in the doorway with a grim expression.

"She came to my office this afternoon."

Dr Graviss gave Liz an expectant look. "Why would you do that?"

"I told him about the baby."

Dr Graviss looked intrigued. "Which would explain why I got a call that you two were in here, arguing."

They both winced. The hospital, the place where they worked, really hadn't been the best place for their revelations.

"Were we that loud?" Liz asked, hoping they hadn't been.

"You were."

"Great." Adam exhaled, ran his fingers through his already ruffled hair. "Just great."

"Why don't you call it a night? Give yourselves some time to let the news sink in. You can talk in the morning." Dr Graviss exchanged glances with Adam. "Or, better yet, you can discuss this tomorrow afternoon once Liz is at home."

"I'm being released tomorrow?"

"That's the plan."

"Good," Adam told his friend, ignoring her completely. "I'll take Liz back to my place for a few days while she recuperates."

Was he insane? There was no way she was going to his place. Not after all the deceptions that had been between them. She'd never trust him again, would always wonder what else he was hiding from her, would always recall that he'd wanted her to abort their baby. *Because of a three to five percent chance.*

Didn't he realize that meant there was a ninety-five to ninety-seven percent chance their baby would be perfect?

"No," she said firmly. "I'm not going to your place. Or anywhere with you for that matter."

"You're going to need someone to help you for a couple of weeks." Adam crossed his arms.

"Kelly or Mona will stay with me at night. Sara—" her grandfather's hired nurse "—will stay with me any night they can't. I've already asked her about doing so, although I haven't given her any dates as I wasn't sure when I'd be discharged." She glanced toward Dr Graviss to make sure he was catching this. She wanted to go home. Wished she were home in her own bed right now. That she could tend her grandfather's roses and talk with him, tell him everything that had happened. How she wished he were here to talk to.

"Honestly, though," she continued before she became teary, "I'd be fine on my own. Other than a trip to the bathroom, I shouldn't have any reason to be out of bed during the night and if I needed someone during the day, I have a phone."

"You need someone with you in case of an emergency. What if your house caught fire and you couldn't get out?"

"Ever the optimist," she accused with another strong dose of sarcasm. "But if that happened, you could count it as your lucky day. You wouldn't have anything to worry about any more, would you?"

His face paled and remorse hit her.

"OK, that's enough, you two," Dr Graviss interrupted, looking disgusted at them both. "Adam, it's time to go."

He appeared ready to argue, but Dr Graviss stood his ground.

Adam didn't look at her, just sounded resigned. "Fine, I'll go, but I'll be by in the morning to pick you up."

"I'm not going with you, Adam," she tossed out as the door closed behind him.

Like she'd go anywhere with someone who'd trusted her so little, who'd deceived her so greatly, who'd thought she'd toss aside their baby.

CHAPTER TWELVE

"You're manipulating me, Dr Graviss. That has to be unethical," Liz accused the following morning when Dr Graviss refused to discharge her unless she let Adam drive her home.

"And it wouldn't be unethical to discharge someone who has no way of getting home?" he asked, arching a brow.

"I have a way to get home," she insisted.

"Not until Mona and Kelly finish their shifts."

"Kelly's already asked the charge nurse if she can take me home during her lunch-break."

"You know she's not supposed to leave the hospital while on duty," Dr Graviss reminded her.

"You're just doing this because Adam is your friend."

Dr Graviss shrugged. "You're my friend, too, Liz. And my patient. I have to do what's best for you. If you want to go home this morning, Adam is your ride."

"I'll call a taxi."

"I'm not going to release my patient to a taxi driver."

"You can't do this," she accused.

"Actually, I can."

"Why would you want to? You're the one who forbade Adam from coming anywhere near me. Why would you try to force us together now?"

"Because Adam was in a place where he couldn't see straight, and every time he was with you he dug a deeper hole, pushed you further away, even though it was the last thing he wanted. He needed some time to come to terms with what was happening to him. You needed time to heal without a stressful confrontation. You're pregnant and were in a serious car crash. The last thing you needed was a major blow-up between you and Adam."

"You think that's not what's going to happen if he drives me home today?"

"He loves you, Liz." Dr Graviss gave her a beseeching look. "He's been going through his own inner hell. Cut him some slack."

"Loves me? Ha. If so, he has a funny way of showing it."

"You have to put yourself in his shoes, Liz. In his warped way, Adam thought he was doing what was best for you."

"You're just saying that because you're his friend," she accused, frustrated by the way she was being pushed into a corner. "Well, he was wrong. All he did was hurt me over and over when he should have been honest with me, told me what was going on so we could face it together."

"He knows that." But it wasn't Dr Graviss who spoke. Adam stood in the doorway, a bouquet of brightly colored flowers in his hands.

"Adam." Dr Graviss glanced at the flowers and shook his head with a wry grin. "I'm going to check on something in the ER. I'll be back by later to see what the plan is so I can write discharge orders." He gave Liz a pointed look. "Or not."

Liz and Adam watched Dr Graviss leave the room.

"He can't do that, you know," Liz said the moment the door closed. "I'm going to complain to the hospital board. He can't blackmail me into letting you take me home. That just isn't right."

Adam's mouth twisted, but he didn't comment, just walked on into Liz's hospital room. He set the flowers down on the tray next to her bed and Liz fought looking at them. She didn't want his flowers. Not now.

"I'm off work the rest of the week, Liz. Next week, too. You may as well let me bring you home and help you. Considering the circumstances, it's the least I can do."

"I don't want your help. Or your pity."

"I thought that was my line," he said softly, startling Liz.

She closed her eyes. She didn't want to fight with Adam. Well, maybe a small part of her did. After weeks of nothing but his avoidance she had so much pent-up emotions that she wanted to lash out at him. He'd deceived her, not trusted her, wanted her to destroy their baby. Any emotions she vented would be filled with anger, hurt, and hatred.

"You should go."

"I'm not going anywhere. Not unless you're with me."

"This is ridiculous, Adam. You avoid me for weeks and now you plan to camp out on my doorstep? Get a life."

"That's what I'm trying to do, but you're not co-operating."

Stunned, she glared at him. "This isn't going to work, you know."

"What?"

"Whatever this is that you're doing."

"I want you back, Liz. I want you to forgive me for not telling you about my MS. I want your love back."

Liz wanted to scream, to throw something at him. Her gaze fell on her bouquet. No, the flowers wouldn't make enough impact on his thick skull to be worth throwing them at him.

"You can't just take back what you've done over the past month, Adam. You can't change the way you've treated me, can't take back the wall you threw between us. It's there and it won't go away."

"I know I can't take back the past month, Liz. Maybe I don't even want to, because the past month has made me realize a lot of things."

That got her attention. "What kind of things?"

"Things like when I was hurting I should have turned to you instead of turning inside out."

She didn't speak. Yes, what he was saying made her heart sing, but words were cheap. Actions spoke much louder and his actions over the past month had screamed that he hadn't trusted her with his heart, with knowledge of his pain, that he had wanted to abort their baby.

"That what everything boils down to," he continued. "You're what matters most to me, Liz. I need you in my life. Otherwise I'm only existing, not living. Not really."

Words. Just cheap words, she reminded herself, even as she felt her heart melting.

"Let me take you home today." He moved closer to her bed. "Let me take care of you, Liz. Give me a second chance. If you still feel the same by the time you're back on your feet, I'll step away or whatever it is you want from me."

"Why are you doing this?"

"I told you," he said solemnly. "Because I want you back."

"Why? Because of my crash? Because of the baby? Why?"

"Because of you."

"Me?"

"I love you, Liz."

How dared he tell her that now? Like this? Especially as he didn't mean it?

Since they were within reach, she picked up the bouquet and threw them at him as hard as she could. The plastic crinkled loudly as the bouquet smacked into him. "Get out," she practically screamed. "Get out of here and don't come back. I'd rather rot in this hospital than to go home with you."

When the time came for Liz to be discharged, she couldn't believe Kelly abandoned her to Adam. Her friend hadn't even looked her in the eyes when she'd come into her room and said she wasn't going to be able to drive Liz home after all.

There was a conspiracy going on and everyone seemed to be in on it.

Did no one care that she just wanted some peace? To go home and absorb everything that had happened and figure out what she wanted for her future?

Not Adam.

Not after everything that had happened. But, still,

there were things she had to figure out. After all, he was the father of her baby.

She slid her hand over her belly. If only Gramps was still alive so she could tell him about the wonderful life growing inside her. Then again, perhaps Gramps would see her baby as a mistake. Just like she'd been her parents' mistake.

No, Gramps had never seen her as a mistake.

He'd been the only one.

Once upon a time she'd believed Adam saw her as someone special, too, but he definitely saw her as a mistake these days, despite his declaration that morning.

He didn't love her, was just confused over everything that had happened, including her pregnancy.

Between her car crash and pregnancy, Adam was trapped.

He felt responsible for her, and as she refused to have an abortion he felt responsible for their baby, too. Saying he loved her was Adam's way of being responsible, trying to take charge of what he considered a bad situation.

She'd like nothing more than to avoid him. Since everyone she called seemed to suddenly be busy, she had no choice but to let Adam drive her if she wanted to go home. She wanted to go home. Desperately.

Kelly helped Liz into a wheelchair, helped position her leg on the leg rest, and gathered Liz's accumulated belongings.

"You know this is wrong?" she asked Kelly, causing a blush to settle on her friend's cheeks.

"What?"

Liz rolled her eyes.

Adam took the plastic hospital bag from Kelly, but she shook her head. "You push Liz, and I'll push the cart with her things."

Her things included the bouquet of flowers that Liz had wanted to throw away, but Kelly had found a vase for them and salvaged it. Some of the stems were a bit the worse for wear and there were a few missing petals, but overall the bouquet was still beautiful.

Liz averted her gaze. She didn't want reminders of Adam's pledge of love. She didn't believe him. Didn't even believe that he believed he loved her.

"Make him squirm, but keep an open mind," Kelly whispered into her ear when they reached the SUV pulled up at the curb.

Liz's eyes widened. Was that what Kelly thought she was doing? Making Adam squirm? She and her friend were going to have a long talk this evening when she came by.

Once settled into the back seat of the car, Liz leaned her head against the plush seat. She didn't want Adam to squirm, didn't want him to feel trapped, didn't want anything from him.

She honestly wasn't sure what the answers were. She was pregnant by a man who didn't love her but felt obligated to do the right thing. How far would he go with that?

She turned her face into the car seat, not liking her fate but knowing she'd survive. A fresh whiff of new-car smell hit her.

"Whose car did you borrow? This looks brand-new."

He seemed surprised that she'd spoken to him. She hadn't since she'd attacked him with his flowers. "It is new."

What he was saying registered.

"You bought a new car?" The entire time she'd known him he'd driven his sporty little two-seater. Why would he buy this roomy, luxurious sports utility vehicle? She wiggled in the seat she sat in and realized the luxurious design hid built-in child seats. Her heart pitter-pattered in her chest. "When?"

"This morning. Your wheelchair wouldn't fit in my car," he explained so matter-of-factly she could have screamed.

She'd assumed he'd borrowed the vehicle, as he had the truck they'd hauled her grandfather's equipment in. How ironic she was using many of the same items she'd given to the assisted living facility?

"You didn't have to buy a new vehicle. For that matter, you didn't have to take me home. I had a way until you so gallantly—" she almost choked on her own words "—stepped in."

"It's really not a big deal, Liz. I wanted to buy a new vehicle, so I did."

Money wasn't the issue for Adam it had always been for her but, still, this was too much. He shouldn't have bought a new car because of her.

"Besides," he continued, "your old car was totaled and you'll need something to drive once you're able to."

A fresh wave of anger welled within her.

"Uh-uh. I'm not driving your car." She shook her finger at him. "You are not going to take over my life,

Adam. What happened today was an aberration. I'm not going to be manipulated into doing what you want me to do over and over, got it? Butt out of my life."

Since Adam wasn't sure how to respond to her outburst he opted to keep his attention on the road.

He supposed he should be grateful Liz was talking to him at all. She didn't want to be in his car or anywhere near him.

Surprisingly, her friends had pushed her into coming with him. So had Larry and Dr Bell. He hadn't asked anyone to force Liz to accept his ride but that's what they'd all done.

He wasn't complaining. He'd do whatever it took to get her to spend time with him, to listen to him, to realize he wanted to make up for his mistakes.

For the time being, Adam chose not to tell Liz that she wouldn't be driving his car, that he'd had the title put in her name that morning. He wanted to take care of her, planned to spend the rest of his life doing just that.

The remainder of the ride to her place was quiet. Never in their relationship had Adam struggled with what to say to Liz, never could he recall feeling awkward with her before her grandfather's death, but he did now. Horribly awkward.

She sat in the car while he got her bag and flowers. He carried the items to the house and let himself in with the key she'd given him months ago. Leaving the front door open, he returned to the car and got Liz's wheelchair out of the back of the SUV. Despite the balmy day, the frame chilled him to the bone.

Would he ever be able to grasp the cold metal of a

wheelchair and not wonder if someday he'd be forced to use one?

But he didn't have time to dwell on what-ifs. Liz sat in the SUV, waiting for him. If she could have managed getting out and into the house by herself, she'd have been long gone. When he opened her car door, she slid her arms around his neck and let him lift her into the waiting wheelchair.

He swallowed at how precious she felt in his arms.

Even with the cast, she was so light he could have carried her into the house. From the stiff way she touched him he knew that the less time they had to touch, the happier she'd be. So he placed her in the wheelchair and pushed her into the house that had been made handicap-accessible years ago for Gramps.

The fact Liz didn't want to touch him cut deeply, but it wasn't anything he didn't deserve. It wasn't anything he hadn't attempted to achieve prior to her crash.

"Thank you," she murmured when he'd settled her on the love seat and propped a couple of pillows beneath her cast to keep it elevated.

"Can I get you something to drink? A snack?"

"I don't even know if there are any groceries here, but I'm not hungry." She shook her head, folded her hands in her lap and closed her eyes, as if dismissing him. "You can go now."

It looked like he'd got what he'd thought he wanted. Liz was apparently finished with him. "I stocked the fridge and cabinets before I picked you up from the hospital."

Adam had gone grocery shopping? Didn't his housekeeper normally do that for him? "Flowers, car, and grocery shopping? My, oh, my, you have had a busy morning."

Adam bit his tongue. It would be so easy to spit out a snappy comeback to Liz's snide remarks. Too easy. Which was what she was going for.

"More so than you'd ever imagine."

He'd been doing a lot of thinking about the future and he'd come to a conclusion. He'd given in his medical leave from the hospital. Until his MS improved, until Liz improved, he wouldn't be returning to his practice.

He wanted his baby to have his name, wanted Liz to have his name when their baby was born.

But she wasn't ready for a proposal. She needed to know he was sincere first. He understood that and would spend however long it took to prove himself to her.

"We left the hospital before they served lunch, so I'll fix something."

"Don't bother. I'm not hungry."

"No bother. You can eat whenever you're ready."

Not only had he bought groceries, but he'd gone by the mom and pop diner he and Liz loved and brought back take-out, along with extra dessert.

When he set the plate of food in front of Liz, she glanced at it, then up at him, a torrent of emotions crossing her face. "Banana pudding?"

"And chicken noodle soup." He gestured to the bowl with the stack of crackers to the side. "I know you've still not been keeping a lot in your stomach."

She seemed lost for words. Perhaps a good thing since everything she'd said to him so far today had been hostile.

"Have you had much morning sickness?"

She groaned. "I really don't want to have this conversation, Adam."

He shouldn't have pressed, but he wanted her to open up to him so badly. "What do you want, Liz?"

"I've already told you." She pinned him beneath her golden gaze. "I want you to leave."

Kelly shook her head as she helped Liz settle onto the love seat in the barren living room of her house. Her foot was propped up on pillows and a wheeled walker sat next to the sofa.

Kelly had come by at the end of her shift and helped Liz to the bathroom, helped her sponge bathe.

Just being clean and in her own clothes made Liz feel more human, more like her old self.

"Where's Adam?"

"He left while you were in the bathroom. Said he had to run a few errands," Kelly said.

"Good. I've been telling him to leave all day. Glad he finally took a hint."

Kelly winced. "Are you sure about this, Liz? Maybe you should give him a chance. It can't have been easy these past few weeks between Gramps's death, being diagnosed with MS, the problems with the board and May's surgery. Adam's been through a lot."

"And I haven't?" Liz asked. "Whose side are you on, anyway?"

Kelly checked the positioning of Liz's leg, rearranged the pillows until she liked the angle and then gave Liz the remote control to the small television set.

"Yours, of course, but that doesn't mean I can't see things from Adam's point of view."

"I thought you wanted to kick him."

"I do, but everyone makes mistakes."

"He wants me to have an abortion, Kelly. That's a bit more than just making a mistake, don't you think?"

"Have you talked to him about that? About why he feels that way?"

She already knew the reason. At least, the one he'd given. "He worries the baby will also have MS."

"A realistic concern."

"So what if our baby did? I'd love him or her anyway. Why can't he?"

"Liz, the baby is real to you. You've heard the heartbeat, felt the changes within your body. You caught Adam by surprise. Did you really expect his gut reaction to be joy when he feels so uncertain about his future already? At any point, did Adam actually say he couldn't love your baby?"

"I think from the moment he said it wasn't too late for an abortion, asking about whether or not he could love this baby was a moot point."

"Liz, he loves you."

She shook her head, ignoring the memory of Adam telling her just that this morning. "He's just saying that because he feels responsible and thought that would win my forgiveness."

"Have you ever thought that maybe you should forgive him?"

"This isn't a matter of forgiveness, Kelly. I don't trust Adam. How can any couple have a relationship when there's no trust?"

"If you say so." Kelly sighed. "Just make sure you aren't being stubborn because of pride or because you're afraid of getting hurt again. I don't want you to make the same mistakes Adam's made."

"Which are?"

"Not having enough faith in your feelings for each other."

"My point exactly." Liz sighed, hoping her broken heart didn't show. "We don't trust each other."

CHAPTER THIRTEEN

THE next morning Liz flicked through the television channels. Nothing was on, of course. She'd already discovered that while in the hospital and there she'd had a lot more channel options than her basic home package.

Kelly had stayed the night, along with an unwanted house guest who'd refused to leave despite Liz asking him to. But Kelly was on duty today and had gone to work a couple of hours ago, first making sure Liz was settled on the sofa and had everything within easy reach. Walker. Remote. Bottled water. A package of peanut butter and crackers. Her cellphone.

Even a couple of magazines.

Adam had left with Kelly, asking her to drop him off at his place to pick up some items.

She'd flipped through the magazines, nibbled on crackers, did another run through of the various television programs, but nothing caught her interest.

Liz was bored. At least at the hospital she'd had people coming in and out of her room. Had noises and pages and such to distract her from the quiet.

Here it was silent except for the sound of a neighbor

doing early morning yard work. Must be her next door neighbor because the noise from the mower sounded really close. Mrs James must have hired someone to come do her lawn.

Perhaps she could get his name and number because her own yard was knee-high in grass. Not to mention that her grandfather's rosebushes were in desperate need of some TLC. Her grandfather would roll over in his grave if he saw the dead blossoms needing to be pruned, saw the weeds sprouting, saw the aphids that no doubt nibbled on tender new buds.

When she next heard the sound of a mower, the buzz sounded so close that she didn't believe it was next door.

Someone was doing her yard.

Preparing herself for the pain that standing caused, she positioned her walker so she could use it to help her get to her feet. Without putting pressure on her bad ankle, she managed to get up. Slowly, she made her way to her front door.

Along with the shiny new SUV, the truck Adam had borrowed to deliver Gramps's belongings to the nursing home was parked in her driveway. The tailgate was down and a mower sat next to the truck.

Adam had stopped and was stooped over, pulling the weeds that had sprung up in the rose garden.

How dared he?

If she could have managed to get down the steps, she would have gone to give him a piece of her mind. She didn't want him doing her yard work.

Or pulling weeds out of her rose garden.

Kelly's warning flashed through her mind.

No, she was not being stubborn. Was not just reacting

out of fear or hurt. She'd given her heart to Adam on a silver platter and he'd trampled it. There was no going back for them. They'd had their shot and blown it.

Emotion spurred her on and, keeping her weight balanced on her good foot and one head gripping her walker, Liz pushed the front door open. "Get out of my grandfather's roses."

Adam pulled more grass from the mulched ground, before glancing at her. "You shouldn't be up."

"Dr Bell told me to get up and move around as much as I felt like, just so long as I kept my weight off my bad leg." She swung her cast around in a little spin.

Adam brushed the dirt from his fingers and straightened from his crouched position.

She angled her walker out the door, supported herself with her arms, and took a step onto the porch.

Adam practically leapt beside her. "You're going to fall. If you want to come outside, let me help you."

"I don't need your help."

"Quit being so stubborn, Liz."

"Why does everyone keep accusing me of being stubborn?" she asked in exasperation.

"You're kidding, right?" he asked with a sheepish grin.

Liz didn't take the bait. He couldn't charm her with that devastating grin. "Fine. Help me. After being in the hospital so long, I want some fresh air. Help me to the swing?"

Without another word, Adam swooped her into his arms and carried her to the wooden swing. Paint peeled from the edges of each slat, revealing the multiple coats of paint that had been applied over the years.

"I didn't mean this kind of help," she protested, wondering why he still hadn't put her down in the swing. She didn't like being in his arms. Didn't want to be in his arms. Much.

But he did smell wonderfully male, felt wonderfully male.

"Then you should be more specific, Liz," he warned. "Because I'm going to take you into my arms every chance I get."

"Don't say that."

"Why not? It's true."

"You are absolutely the most confusing man I've ever met," she complained.

"Which is why you love me so much."

Adam knew he'd pushed his luck by the sour look that came over Liz's face. Actually, she'd already had a fairly sour expression, but she wrinkled her nose and glared.

But she didn't deny his claim. Which gave him hope.

He sat down in the swing, keeping Liz in his lap with her feet on the opposite side of the swing.

"Put me down."

"Can't."

"Why not?"

He gestured to the opposite side of the swing. "There wouldn't be any place for me to sit."

Liz followed his gaze to her feet and wiggled her bare toes. "You know I'm not going to be helpless for ever, right? That I'm going to be walking on my own again soon and you aren't going to be able to boss me around like this?"

"I know. That's why I figure I'd better make the most

of it while you're at my mercy." He hugged her to him, breathed in her familiar scent. "I love you, Liz."

She pushed against his chest. "Stop saying that."

"Never. I'm going to tell you every day for the rest of our lives."

She rolled her eyes. "Why?"

"Because it's true."

"How can you say that when you've spent the past month pushing me away when I needed you so much? When you don't want me pregnant with your baby?"

"Because I was a fool and thought I could do this on my own, Liz. And the truth is I can do it on my own, but I don't want to. Part of me still believes that's selfish as hell because you shouldn't be tied to a man who doesn't know what his future holds."

"None of us know what our future holds," she pointed out, but without the bitterness he'd grown accustomed to hearing over the past twenty-four hours.

"Your accident made me realize that. Each and every day of life is a blessing that should be lived to its fullest."

Adam used his feet to keep them gently moving back and forth. They swung in silence for a long time, Liz eventually relaxing against him.

Although the sun hadn't reached its peak in the sky, he'd worked up a sweat mowing her yard. Fortunately her yard wasn't that large and although his T-shirt clung to him he didn't think he was too gross.

Apparently not as Liz laid her head on his shoulder.

"Tell me about your MS."

His heart sang at her request. "What do you want to know?"

"Everything."

So he told her everything. From the first time he'd noticed his blurry vision, to the tingles in his fingers, to how terrified he'd been when he'd gone blind in his right eye. How he'd thought if he loved her he would end their relationship and let her have a life without being tied to an ill man. How he had struggled with actually letting her go.

"The night you came here that you made love to me, what happened that day, Adam?"

"Dr Winters confirmed my diagnosis." He traced his fingers over her arms, wondering how it could feel so right to dump all this on Liz, to tell her everything in his heart. "Up to that point I'd held out hope that I didn't really have MS and all this would go away."

She twisted her neck to look at him. "You'd been drinking. I could smell it on you and knew something was wrong."

"A little. I needed liquid courage for what I had to do. Thought I had to do."

Her eyes glowed like golden honey. "You came to tell me we were finished?"

"That's what I told myself, because I couldn't face the truth. That I needed you to hold me so I'd know the world hadn't gone completely crazy." Pushing his luck, Adam slid his hand to hers and laced their fingers. "I needed you that night, Liz. I always need you. I know I betrayed your trust, but if you'll forgive me, I'll spend every breath I take re-earning it, proving to you that what we have is real."

She stiffened, but didn't pull away, didn't say anything, and they sat in the swing until the sun was high in the sky and beat down on them.

"I'm ready to go in now." Her purposely aloof voice told him everything. She wasn't ready to forgive him.

He nodded, stood up with her in his arms and carried her into the house. "The sofa or your bedroom?"

Her quick glance at him let Adam know exactly where her mind was. And where it wasn't.

"The sofa."

Adam laid her on the sofa, waited for her to say something, anything, but when she didn't he went outside to get her walker. When he returned, Liz's eyes were shut, but she wasn't asleep, just ignoring him.

While holding her, he'd been hopeful, had thought she might find it in her heart to forgive him. It was too soon. He'd hurt her too badly. But he'd never give up, never let her doubt his feelings for her again. For the rest of his life he'd make sure Liz knew she was what mattered most to him.

He put the walker within her reach, bent and kissed the top of her head. "I love you, Liz, and hope someday you'll trust me enough with your heart, our baby, that you can forgive me."

Through the window, Liz watched Adam work. No matter how hard she tried she couldn't regain her anger.

She wanted to, she realized. Because as long as she stayed angry, that provided a protective shield around her heart. A protective shield she desperately needed.

Listening to Adam talk about his MS, feeling the emotions in every word he said, she understood how he'd felt. Not that she agreed with his reasoning, she didn't. But she understood that he'd wanted to protect her from what he'd seen as his bleak future.

She couldn't deny that her heart belonged to him and she believed he hadn't meant to hurt her.

Understanding didn't bring trust or erase the pain she'd felt. Neither did it change his reaction to learning of her pregnancy.

So where did that leave them?

Adam laughed at the word Liz made up on the Scrabble board. He wasn't sure "Podunk" was a real word or just Southern slang for a tiny, offbeat town. But he let her count it all the same. Seeing her smile was worth getting his butt kicked in a board game.

Two weeks had passed since the morning he'd cut her lawn. Two weeks where Liz no longer attacked him with every word. Two weeks where he did his best to show her how he felt about her. Two weeks where he continued his injections, was getting rest, and with each day that passed he felt a little stronger, a little more in control of his life.

Which could all be attributed to Liz's tentative acceptance of his presence in her house, in her life.

Kelly still came by every day, Mona most days, too, but when Liz needed something that she couldn't manage on her own, she'd ask for his help.

She was getting stronger with each day as well. At her last appointment with Dr Bell he'd told her to get rid of the walker and start using crutches. Before long she'd be recovered and back at work.

Back at work.

That morning Dr Winters released Adam to return to work whenever he felt ready, saying that unless Adam had a worsening of symptoms, he could return to a lighter schedule.

Liz had gone with him to the specialist's office. He'd been surprised but pleased when she'd asked to go.

Actually, he'd decided she'd had her own agenda in going with him. She'd asked about their baby, wanting to know all the statistics, research, and anything she could do to decrease the risk.

He'd sat on the exam table, feeling inadequate, ashamed that he'd done this to her, to their baby.

"Hello." Liz snapped her fingers in front of his face. "It's your go."

"What's your rush?" he teased, wanting to hang onto the peace between them. "You think if you give me too much time I'll figure out a way to win?"

"Right." She laughed. "You've caught me now."

Adam studied the Scrabble board and chose his letters, his word, wondering if fate had caused him to look at his game pieces and see only one possible word to be made from his squares.

He arranged the pieces on the board.

Liz stared first at the word, then at Adam.

The moment stretched awkwardly between them before a tear trickled down her face. "Adam?"

His gaze connected with hers and he hoped she saw everything she was to him. His whole world.

She glanced down at the board, her gaze soaking in the word he'd spelled. "Baby".

"There's something I have to tell you." She leaned forward, her eyes soft, her expression yearning. "I'm pregnant."

Confused, Adam didn't breathe, didn't move. What was she doing? He already knew she was pregnant.

She'd told him in his office during the worst phase

of his life. And he'd blown it. Blown it so badly Liz couldn't forgive him.

Then it hit him.

She was starting over, giving him a second chance to get things right.

His heart swelled with love for her, at this gift she was giving him. "You're pregnant?"

"I know we weren't planning to start a family, and I didn't mean to get pregnant, but I am, and I love this baby very much. Not just because it's mine." She placed her hand over his. "But because it's yours."

Feeling light-headed, he sucked in a breath of air.

"Because I love you, Adam. And, despite there being risks and us having had recent problems, there's nobody else's baby I want. Just yours."

Her words cut into his chest, pierced his heart.

"No matter what your future holds, good health or not, I love you," she whispered. "You, you, and only you. It's the man you are inside who I love. The person who makes me whole."

Adam lifted her hand to his mouth, kissed her fingers. "I don't want to hurt you, Liz. Not ever."

"I know that."

Looking into her eyes, he saw the forgiveness, the reality that she did know that he'd never meant to cause her pain.

"I don't want to burden you." He squeezed her hand, willing her to understand what he was saying. "If a time comes in the future when you need to leave, I'll understand."

She shook her head at him. "Haven't you learned anything these past few weeks? Being without you is what hurts me, Adam." She reached across the coffee-table he'd wedged next to the sofa so they could play their game and tangled her fingers in the fabric of his T-shirt, tugging him toward her. Pushing the game board aside, he slid toward her, stopping only when their faces were millimeters apart. "For the record, I won't understand if you leave me. I didn't understand a month ago, and I won't understand at any point in the future."

"I'm sorry, Liz." If he told her a million times how sorry he was it wouldn't be enough to erase what he'd done to her.

"We're putting that behind us, Adam. It's in the past." She let go of his shirt, smoothed the fabric, and cupped his face. "It's the future that's important. Our future."

Her meaning rang clear and his heart almost burst with his emotions for Liz. No matter what, as long as they were together the future would work itself out. They could face any tribulation. Together.

"I don't deserve you, Liz, but I thank God I have you. I love you." He kissed her, holding her close, knowing that he'd hold onto Liz with all his heart for the rest of his life.

"I'll never leave you. Not so long as you'll have me." She smiled brightly, pressing her lips to his. "Good. Then you're going to be mine for ever."

"Tell me again," he said, moments later, wondering exactly how he'd gotten across the coffee-table and tangled up with Liz on the love seat. Adam slid his hand beneath the waist band of her shorts, rested it against the gentle bump.

Liz's lips curved into a smile. "I'm having your baby."

Adam let out a joyous whoop that had Liz first rolling her eyes, then sniffling, all the while battling laughter.

He looked into her eyes, saw Liz's love for him shining brightly and realized he understood how she felt. He would want to stay by her side no matter what, for richer, for poorer, for good health or bad, for always.

EPILOGUE

SWEAT beaded on Liz's forehead. Never in her life had she felt such intense pain. Not even following her car crash.

Lord, if this baby didn't get here soon she was going to split in half.

"You're doing great, honey," Adam encouraged from beside her, trying to force-feed her another ice chip. Adam's MS had gone into remission and he'd been symptom-free for months now. They both knew that could change in the blink of an eye, but they kept their hearts focused on what mattered most. Each other.

"Just a little while longer and our daughter will be here."

They'd been arguing for weeks on the sex of the baby. Adam saying they were going to have a daughter, Liz insisting the baby was a boy. Neither had found out during her ultrasounds and had asked the radiologist to edit any clips that revealed the sex as they truly didn't want to know until delivery.

"Luther Jacob Cline—" named after Gramps "—will be very upset when he learns his father kept insisting he was a girl. Poor kid might develop a complex."

"I'm telling you Elizabeth Ann—" named after Liz, as well as Adam's mother "—is who's arriving today."

Another contraction hit Liz, tightening her stomach into a hard knot. "Whoever is in here, I wish they'd hurry."

An hour later, Liz gave birth to a round-faced little boy. She'd never seen Adam look happier, more proud, more loving, and she knew he'd keep the vows they'd made to one another the very week Dr Bell had OK'd her to put weight on her ankle to hobble down the aisle sans crutches.

No matter what their future held, she and Adam would face it together.

"He's gorgeous, Liz. The most precious baby," Adam cooed, cuddling their son in his arms from where he sat next to her on the hospital bed.

Liz glanced into her son's face, watched him attempt to suck on his fist. "Our baby. If only Gramps were here…"

Adam took her hand, lifted it to his lips, and placed a kiss. "He's watching from heaven, Liz. You know he is and that he's proud of you."

Yes, she did know that and from somewhere above she'd swear she heard Gramps say, "Good job, Liza girl. Good job."

Passion. Power. Suspense.
It's time to fall under the spell of Nora Roberts.

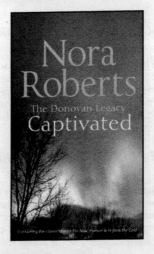

For the latest script of his blockbuster horror film, Nash Kirkland tracks down self-proclaimed witch Morgana Donovan and sceptically demands the secrets of her imaginary craft.

Nash is stunned to discover that he is equally mystified by and attracted to Morgana. Either he is being driven mad or Morgana is telling the truth about her powers. And the most important choice Nash will ever make depends on getting the answer right.

This is the first volume in Nora Roberts' spellbinding *The Donovan Legacy*.

Available 2nd January 2009

Passion. Power. Suspense.
It's time to fall under the spell of Nora Roberts.

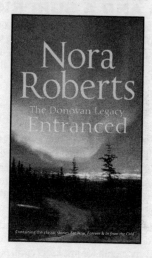

A missing child. A desperate mother.
A private investigator running out of time.

Reluctantly, Mel Sutherland had to accept Sebastian Donovan's aid. She was cynical about his powers and suspicious of his motives. But as the clock ticked, Sebastian unfailingly knew how to follow the abductor's tracks and Mel had to make up her mind. Was Sebastian's gift real? Or was something far more sinister at work?

This is the second volume in Nora Roberts' spellbinding *The Donovan Legacy*.

Available 6th February 2009

FREE

4 BOOKS AND A SURPRISE GIFT!

We would like to take this opportunity to thank you for reading this Mills & Boon® book by offering you the chance to take FOUR more specially selected titles from the Medical™ series absolutely FREE! We're also making this offer to introduce you to the benefits of the Mills & Boon® Book Club™—

* ★ FREE home delivery
* ★ FREE gifts and competitions
* ★ FREE monthly Newsletter
* ★ Books available before they're in the shops
* ★ Exclusive Mills & Boon Book Club offers

Accepting these FREE books and gift places you under no obligation to buy; you may cancel at any time, even after receiving your free shipment. Simply complete your details below and return the entire page to the address below. You don't even need a stamp!

YES! Please send me 4 free Medical books and a surprise gift. I understand that unless you hear from me, I will receive 6 superb new titles every month for just £2.99 each, postage and packing free. I am under no obligation to purchase any books and may cancel my subscription at any time. The free books and gift will be mine to keep in any case.

M9ZEE

Ms/Mrs/Miss/Mr.................................Initials ....
                                                                        BLOCK CAPITALS PLEASE

Surname ....

Address ....

....

....Postcode ....

Send this whole page to:
The Mills & Boon Book Club, FREEPOST CN81, Croydon, CR9 3WZ